John Christopher Schwab

The Revolutionary History of Fort Number Eight

on Morris Heights, New York City

John Christopher Schwab

The Revolutionary History of Fort Number Eight
on Morris Heights, New York City

ISBN/EAN: 9783337390914

Printed in Europe, USA, Canada, Australia, Japan

Cover: Foto ©Andreas Hilbeck / pixelio.de

More available books at **www.hansebooks.com**

THE

REVOLUTIONARY HISTORY

·OF·

Fort Number Eight

ON

MORRIS HEIGHTS, NEW YORK CITY

BY

JOHN CHRISTOPHER SCHWAB

PRIVATELY PRINTED

1897

NEW HAVEN, CONN.

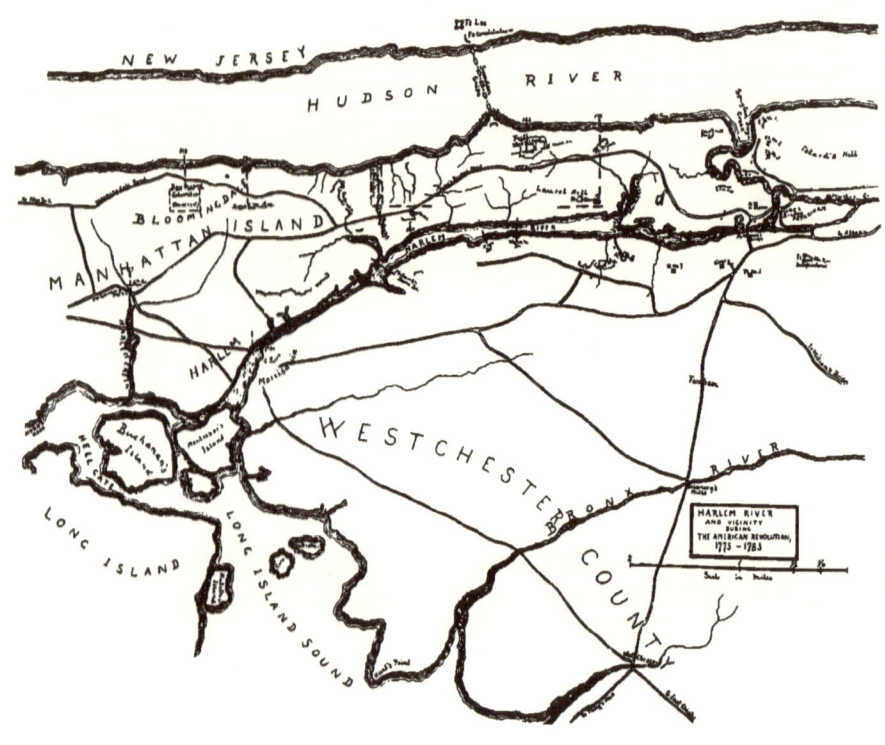

THE MANOR OF FORDHÁM

AND

THE ARCHER FAMILY.

The Manor of Fordham, consisting of 1,253 acres, was part
of the Indian lands known as Kekeshick or Keskeskick, bor-
dering on the Harlem River, and was owned by the sachems
Feequemeck, Rechgawar and Packanmans, who conveyed it—
the first sale of land by the Indians in Westchester County—
to the Dutch West India Company ("de Hollandsche Westin-
dische Compagnie") in 1639, thirteen years after the settle-
ment of New Amsterdam.[1]

Adriaen Van der Donck, the first lawyer who came to New
Netherland, owned Fordham and Yonkers as Patroon, by purchase from the company on August 3, 1646.[2] He built his
house on the present Van Cortlandt Parade Ground, and also
a saw-mill in the so-called "Saw-Mill" or "Saw Kill Val-
ley," and died in 1665. Yonkers is named after him (Jonk-
heer).[3] His widow, Mary, married Hugh O'Neale of Maryland, and deeded part of the manor to her brother-in-law,
Elias Doughty, on October 30, 1666, some weeks after Governor Nichols had confirmed Hugh and Mary's title to their
land, Van der Donck's purchase having been made under
the Dutch *régime* before 1664. One part of the manor she
sold to John Archer on March 1, 1667, and another part,
described as eighty acres upland and thirty meadow land, to
the same Archer on September 18, 1667.[4]

On application to the English government, letters patent
were issued to John Archer on November 13, 1671. He was
to pay a customary annual quit rent, to consist of twenty
bushels of good pears. The document describes the tract of
land as lying to the eastward of Harlem River "where ye
new dorp or village is erected known by the name of Fordham."[5]

The Archer family was of English origin, the name going back to the time of the Crusades. Fulbert l'Archer is mentioned as having emigrated to England with William the Conqueror. Some six hundred years later John Archer pushed on from Warwickshire to the new world, settling in Westchester County about 1654.[1] Having purchased the Manor of Fordham, he became its "landheer," and evidently made full use of the authority granted him, for when in 1673 the Dutch dominion over New York was for a short time restored, the inhabitants of Fordham petitioned the government for relief from the harsh treatment of their lord.[2]

A few years later, in November, 1676, John Archer got into difficulties of another kind, and mortgaged his land to the wealthy Mynheer Cornelius Steenwyck to secure a loan of 24,000 guilders seawant. The loan was not paid, and John Archer forfeited the manor to Steenwyck, or rather to his widow, on October 16, 1685.[3] She married again, and with her second husband, Dominie Henricus Selyns, conveyed the land on January 10, 1694, to Colonel Nicholas Bayard, Captain Isaac Vermilyee, Jacob Rockloysen and John Harpendick, overseers of the Dutch Reformed Church, which was fully organized in Fordham by the Collegiate Dutch Church of New York (which still exists) on May 11, 1696, and built a church north of the present road to Fordham Landing on the land of Mr. Moses Devoe—the Dutch Presbyterians (Dutch Reformed) were most numerous in Westchester County at the time.[4]

Half a century later, in December, 1753, this church was authorized to and did sell one hundred and eight acres of its land to Daniel Seacord (or Sicard) of Yonkers, who twelve years later, on October 14, 1766, sold seventy acres of the tract, which included the present site of Fort Number Eight, to Benjamin Archer for £630.[5] Thus part of the property of the original John Archer passed back to his grandson Benjamin, who built the family homestead, known later as "Colonel DeLancey's Headquarters," a hundred yards north of Mr. G. L. Dashwood's place (the Berkeley Oval).[6]

This Benjamin Archer, Senior, and his wife Esther deeded half their property to their son Benjamin, Junior, on February 13, 1769, for £330. They left two sons, the above Benjamin

Junior and John, and two daughters, Sarah and Rachel. The former married Jacob Collard, the latter James Crawford—of the latter four only James Crawford could write his name. Being provided with husbands or otherwise, the two sisters and John deeded their share of their father's property on April 12, 1786, to their eldest brother Benjamin.[12] In 1807 (December 12) this Benjamin Archer, Junior, died, and directed in his will that his land should be divided between his two sons, William and Samuel D., when the latter came of age, which was accordingly done in 1817. The third son and the daughters received legacies of money and some feather beds. The older brother again increased his talents by acquiring Samuel D.'s land on October 29, 1835.[13] His home was east of the Croton Aqueduct opposite the entrance to Mr. Mali's place. On March 17, 1857, he sold 7 and 951/1000 acres of it through Mr. James Punnett to Catherine Elizabeth, wife of the late Mr. Gustav Schwab.[14] The Archer family moved to near New Rochelle, where they still are to be found.

To return to the earlier history of the Archers : As was the case in many American families when the Revolution broke out, the Archers were divided in their allegiance to King George and to the American cause. Caleb and Gabriel Archer signed the declaration to support the King at the White Plains Convention of April 13, 1775.[15] Among the other signers were Levi Devoe and such familiar names as Purdy and Valentine. In the following year the Loyalist Declaration of October 16, 1776, was signed by John Archer. He was in good company, for with him were the Rev. Dr. S. Auchmuty and Rev. Charles Inglis of Trinity Church, later Bishop of Nova Scotia, Samuel Bayard, Colonel William Bayard, Henry Brevoort, James Des Brosses, Alexander Leslie, headmaster of King's College (now Columbia University), Frederic Rhinelander, Leonard Lispenard and Augt Van Cortlandt.[16] The Archer we are particularly interested in, however, namely Benjamin Junior, joined the "rebel" army as a private in a company organized in West Farms and the Manor of Fordham under the command of Captain Nicholas Berrian, a neighbor of the Archer family. Archer had signed with others the petition to form it as a company of militia on September 5, 1775. The lieutenants were Gilbert Taylor and Daniel Devoe ; the ensign,

Benjamin Valentine. Among the other privates we find Peter Bussing, James Archer and some Devoes. Presumably this same James Archer appears in 1778 as ensign in Colonel Samuel Drake's Third (North or Manor of Van Cortlandt) Regiment, and a year later as Second Lieutenant." Other Archers, Anthony, Basal and Mathious, were enrolled in a Yonkers Company September 15, 1775. It is noticeable that they all could write their names on the enlistment rolls, and did not put their mark as so many did."

To properly understand the history of the Revolution in New York, one must bear in mind that most of the respectable and conservative families in and about the city sided with the English. Their devotion to the Church of England, their love of law and order, and their conservative attachment to the old *régime*, under which they had prospered, were decisive." To such Loyalists the destruction of King George's statue on Bowling Green on July 9, 1776," like the Boston Tea Party, were acts of mob violence and vandalism. Peter Elting writes to Richard Varick on June 13, 1776 :" "We had some grand Toory Rides in the City this week . . . . Several of them were handled Verry Roughly Being caried trugh the streets on Rails, there Cloaths Tore from there becks and their Bodies pritty well Mingled with the dust."

One of the most prominent American families that remained loyalist were the DeLanceys. Oliver DeLancey, the brother of Lieutenant Governor James DeLancey, was the senior loyalist officer in the American Revolution. Born in New York in 1717, he died in England in 1785. He was the Colonel of a New York regiment under Abercrombie, and in 1776 was made a brigadier-general in the British army. In 1777 he was attainted of treason, and his estates were confiscated by the State of New York."

His son Oliver and nephew James were both in the British army. Oliver DeLancey, the son, gained a high position. In 1776 he busied himself enlisting loyalists. In July, 1778, he was made a major, and in 1781 a lieutenant-colonel, succeeding Major Andrée as Adjutant-General in that year, and, as such, he signed the orders to evacuate New York in March, 1783. He died in Edinburgh in 1822."

The nephew, James DeLancey, organized and commanded

the famous "Cow-Boys," a corps belonging to the loyalist regiment of his uncle Oliver, with headquarters at Morrisania, which foraged in the neighborhood for the British garrison in New York. He was taken prisoner by the Americans in 1777, and spent a while in the Hartford goal. At the end of the war his estates were confiscated, and he retired to Nova Scotia with many other Tories, where he died in 1800.[24]

These troops under Colonel James DeLancey played a prominent part in the incessant skirmishes in southern Westchester County (as we shall see). Another regiment of loyalists we shall hear of was the First American Regiment, better known as the "Queen's Rangers," which had been raised by Robert Rogers, a Tory of New Hampshire.[25] These "Rangers" were recruited largely from the neighborhood of New York, and were put under the command of Colonel J. G. Simcoe by General Howe on October 15, 1777. After the war, like the other loyalist troops, they were transported to Nova Scotia.[26]

NEW YORK AND THE REVOLUTION.

The city of New York at the outbreak of the Revolution had a population of about 25,000, who lived in the closely built up southern part of Manhattan Island about Fort George (on the site of the present battery), and south of the line passing through Reade Street to the East River and Catherine Street." At the corner of Pearl and Broad Streets stood the famous tavern of Samuel Fraunces, the Delmonico of that time, originally noted for his excellent pickles and preserves, and later as steward of the Presidential mansion." The Swamp Church (corner of Franklin and North William Streets), whose pastor at a later time was Dr. John Christopher Kunze, was standing at the time." The Provincial Secretary's office stood on the western corner of Bowling Green and Whitehall Street, on the site of the present office of Oelrichs and Company."

Westchester County, which at the time was bounded on the south by the Long Island Sound and the Harlem River, is described as "in general rough but fertile, and therefore the farmers run principally on grazing."" Hence, too, the British troops found on the farms a convenient supply of food, to which they were constantly helping themselves during the war, 1776-1783, much to the injury of the inhabitants of that section as we shall see." King's Bridge, the first, and, until Dykeman's (now Farmers') Bridge was built, the only bridge connecting Manhattan Island with the main land, was built and given its name at the end of the 17th century. The first structure was of wood, a little east of its present location (perhaps on the site of the present foot-bridge)." In 1704 a toll of three pence was charged for passing the bridge with a horse. To avoid this and similar charges a new bridge was built on the site of the present Farmers' Bridge by Jacob Dykeman and Johannes Vermilyea, and was named after the former."

As to the roads in use at the time of the Revolution, there is necessarily great uncertainty, owing to the divergence of the maps." A comparison of them, however, gives the following probable result as to the main highways :

From McGowan's Pass (107th Street) and Bloomingdale

(119th Street) a road led through Manhattanville (near the present St. Mary's Church), between the present lines of Amsterdam Avenue and the Boulevard, toward Fort Washington (183d Street and Fort Washington Avenue), passing the house of Colonel Roger Morris (later the Jumel house) on the right,[16] and further on the Blue Bell Tavern, probably on the left.[17] From Fort Washington the road descended toward Inwood between the heights on which Fort Washington and, further north, Fort Tryon, were built on the left, and Laurel Hill on the right, on the northern end of which was the redoubt known later as Fort George (194th Street, between Amsterdam Avenue and the Boulevard). At Inwood, in the neighborhood of the present Presbyterian church, the road turned to the east, passed near the "Century House,"[18] and skirted the Harlem River till it reached King's Bridge. From there it circled to the right, much as it does now, and turned northward along the east bank of the Mosholu Creek toward the Van Cortlandt house, and on to Yonkers or Phillipsburg, as it is generally called, and eventually led to Albany.

A branch of this road crossed the Harlem River over Dykeman's (now Farmers') Bridge, and followed roughly the present line of the road up the steep hill, past the present Dutch church, through Fordham village and Delancey's Mills on the Bronx River (Bronxdale) to Westchester, and finally led to Connecticut. From this road another led to the south from near the present Dutch church along the line of what was later the MacComb's Dam Road near the English Fort Number Eight, and the houses of Benjamin Archer (north of the Berkeley Oval) and Colonel Richard Morris, (in the present garden of his grandson, Lewis G. Morris), to Morrisania (now Mott Haven), and the house of Lewis Morris (still standing near the Third Avenue Bridge), from near which a ferry (established in 1667) crossed to Harlem and a road led northeastward to Westchester.

March 17, 1776, the British forces had been starved out of Boston by the American troops which surrounded them, and, evacuating that town,[19] they set sail for Halifax, and thence later for New York, where, as we know, they met with better success than in Boston, and maintained themselves till the end of the war.

Little had been done to put the city into a state of defence, though Abraham Varick writes on March 28, 1775:[9] "we are and will be so well fortified as to give them a scrag they will not Relish very well." Peter Elting in a letter dated September 12, 1776,[10] was much nearer the truth when he wrote "the town appears to me to be in a Bad state of defence."

As early as January, 1776, General Charles Lee had written to General Washington,[11] to offer to collect volunteers in New England with which to protect New York—he foresaw it would soon be attacked,—and to annoy the Tories, especially on Long Island, where they were numerous. It was useless to apply to the Congress. By Washington's authority Lee at once collected troops in New England, and started for New York from New Haven in the middle of January, 1776, reporting to Washington[12] that Colonel Waterbury had raised a regiment of seven hundred men. The approach of these troops frightened the Colonial authorities in New York, who begged Lee to desist, as they did not wish to provoke hostilities.[13] But Lee continued the movement toward New York by way of Rye, New Rochelle and East Chester,[14] and by February, 1776, some New England troops had arrived in New York ;[15] "Cornel Water Berry whit about 1,000 men . . . . also 500 minet men from New England." "On the 4 Instant in the morning arived General Clinton . . . . the same day arived Generel Lee Whit 300 men it is imbosseble to Describ the convusen that this city was in on account of the Regelers Being Com." On February 7, 1776, General Sterling arrived with 1,000 men from New Jersey.

So far no attempt had been made to fortify New York. General Lee at once drew up plans for fortifications about Hell Gate,[16] and barricades on the streets, especially one on Broadway, two hundred yards north of Bowling Green,[17] and for strong redoubts about King's Bridge, which he as well as Generals Heath and Greene thought of the utmost importance.[18] Many of the cannon were taken from Fort George (the Battery) and carried to King's Bridge, but were found useless. There was a great lack of men to build these fortifications—only 1,700 men composed the garrison of New York on February 29, 1776,[19] the terms of enlistment of most of them were about to expire, and the Congress seemed unable or unwilling to help matters.

General Heath found works being erected in and about New York on his arrival at the end of March, 1776—the Westchester minute men had been building redoubts to command Hell Gate. Soon after, Generals Putnam and Sullivan arrived, and on April 13, Generals Washington and Gates, followed by General Greene with his brigade. The construction of works was hurried on, as it was correctly surmised that the British would soon turn their attention to New York.[51] Little, however, was accomplished before the arrival of the British in July, when Fort Washington was hastily erected.

On June 3, 1776, the tardy Congress, which had been warned by General Lee four months before, realized that New York would be the next point of attack, and decided to reinforce the city with 13,800 militia troops from Pennsylvania, Delaware and Maryland.[52] These soon began to arrive, the Pennsylvania troops under General Thomas Mifflin, who is described as a "bustler" by Major Alexander Graydon, his Aide.[53] Of these Pennsylvania troops the Third battalion was commanded by Colonel John Shee. Later, in September, 1776, he was on furlough, and Lieutenant-Colonel Cadwallader took command.[54] The Fifth Pennsylvania battalion was commanded by Colonel Robert Magaw, whom we shall meet again as the commandant of Fort Washington ([55]). A non-commissioned officer in this battalion, Christopher Weiser, Sergeant in Captain Peter Dickey's Company, interests us. After the war he resided in Buffalo township, Union County, Pennsylvania (in 1792).[56] These raw and undisciplined troops were mostly recruited from Pennsylvania, New Jersey, Delaware and Maryland under officers chiefly from Philadelphia. They reached New York, June 20 to 25, 1776,[57] and were drilled hard during the hot summer about their headquarters at Fort Washington, which they were building; occasionally short marches were made into Westchester County, presumably to replenish their larder.[58] We learn from Graydon's Memoirs[59] that of seventy-three of the Pennsylvania troops, forty-five were natives, twenty were from Ireland, four from England and two from Scotland. General Heath tells us:[60] "They had the appearance of fine troops."

Beside the Pennsylvania troops under General Mifflin, two Massachusetts regiments reached New York during July and August, 1776. One, under Colonel John Glover, left Boston on July 20 and reached New York August 9 ; the other, as we learn from David How's Diary, left Boston July 18 and reached New York August 27, 1776.[⁶]

Six Connecticut regiments arrived in New York about the same time, one of which joined Mifflin's command. They are described in a contemporary Connecticut newspaper as "an exceeding fine Body of Men, well equipped and disciplined."[⁶²]

General Charles Lee, in writing to Edmund Burke in 1774, also mentioned the soldierly bearing of the New England militia, a recent development, he thinks.[⁶] This did not prevent the soldiers from other sections looking down upon those from New England, traces of which feeling are frequent.[⁶⁴]

New York itself furnished, of course, its quota of defenders. Peter Elting writes on July 30, 1776 :[⁶⁵] "Verry few of the inhabitents Remain in town that are not ingaged in the Service." John Varick in a letter dated June 25, 1776[⁶⁶] claims that one quarter of the citizens have turned out as volunteers or by draught. All males between sixteen and sixty years old were subject to the draft.[⁶⁷] Colonel Lasser figures as the colonel of the First New York Independent Foot Company.[⁶⁸] Colonel Drake's Westchester Minute Men—one hundred and eleven privates, nineteen commissioned, and twenty non-commissioned officers—were also on hand to help strengthen the city's defences.[⁶⁹]

The strongest of these fortifications in and about the city was Fort Washington,[⁷⁰] which was built under the direction of Colonel Rufus Putnam by the above Pennsylvania troops on their arrival, and was intended, together with Fort Lee (or Constitution) on the opposite shore of the river, to command the Hudson and prevent the British ascending and cutting off the Americans' connection with New England.[⁷¹] The work of building the fort proceeded slowly, for by August 18, 1776, no cannon were mounted there.[⁷²] Graydon, whose battalion served under Colonel Cadwallader, complains that the fort's position was a weak one. It had no water, no ditch, and there was higher ground near by.[⁷³]

Other American fortifications built at this time were earth-

works—later called Fort Tryon—on the northern end of the
ridge on which Fort Washington was situated (between 195th
and 198th Streets), and overlooking Inwood." On Laurel
Hill, overlooking the Harlem River, was also erected a redoubt,
later called Fort George by the British." The earthworks
were still extant in 1890, but have now been effaced by a
resort called "Fort George Park." Below on the King's
Bridge Road a strong four-gun battery was built." On the
northern end of the ridge on Manhattan Island was built Cock
Hill Fort, and a series of redoubts, numbered one, two and
three, on the slope north of Spuyten Duyvil Creek, on the
site of the old Indian fortress Nipinicksen."

At the suggestion of Generals Heath and Greene, and under
the direction of Colonel Rufus Putnam, the chief engineer of
the American army, Fort Independence was built by two
battalions of Pennsylvania troops and some militia. It is still
standing on the site of Mr. W. O. Giles' house (once the
residence of Mr. D. L. Turner), west of Sedgwick Avenue and
near the entrance to Van Cortlandt Park. Some cannon still
remain there." It is noticeable that the then owner of the
place, General Richard Montgomery, was not paid for his land,
and his executor in 1788 petitioned for reimbursement."

To insure Fort Washington's control of the Hudson,
obstructions were placed in the river between that fort and
Fort Lee. But to no purpose ; for when the British arrived,
two of their ships with three tenders forced their way up the
river on July 12, 1776, to Tappan Bay, exchanging shots
with the American forts." Three months before two English
men-of-war had appeared in New York harbor, but had kept
out of range of the American guns."

The British fleet, in fact, had been sighted on June 25, 1776,
had anchored at Sandy Hook on June 28 and 29, and
debarked their troops on Staten Island on July 2 and 3."
General Howe, the commander-in-chief of the expedition,
arrived some days later in the man-of-war "Eagle" (which
ship we shall meet again), and established himself on Staten
Island on July 12."

Sir William Howe was born August 10, 1729, and served
under General Wolfe at Quebec in 1759. He distinguished
himself in this New York campaign—he was made a Knight of

the Bath—returned to England before the end of the war, and died July 12, 1814."

In the campaign before us General Howe commanded the 16th and 17th Regiments of Dragoons, 1,105 footguards, twenty-three regiments of ten companies each, the 42d or Royal Highlanders, the 71st or Frazer's Battalion, six companies of artillery, six battalions of marines, and the Hessian infantry and artillery which arrived later, a total force of 33,614." Opposed to them in and about New York were General Washington's troops, numbering perhaps 23,000 men."

After a seven weeks' stay on Staten Island, the British crossed to Long Island, landed near Gravesend Bay on August 22, and prepared for the battle of the following week."

In the meantime the Americans had been aroused to realizing the dangers the city was in. On August 8, General Clinton was ordered to make new levies in Dutchess, Orange, Ulster and Westchester Counties, to proceed at once to strengthen the fortifications about King's Bridge, and to prevent the British occupying those positions in the rear of the American army and cutting off its communication with Albany." A week later seven hundred men had been collected in those posts." On August 17, General Washington put General Heath—who had been made a major-general by Congress a week before—in command of the troops at the north end of the island, specifically including those in Fort Washington and Fort Independence, "and a number of other works" (described above)," which he was familiar with from personal observation.

General Heath at once took command with headquarters at King's Bridge, from where he writes to Washington on August 23, advising the building of a floating bridge across the Harlem River. He was also busy reconnoitering, and obtained Lieutenant Preston from General H. Knox to superintend the mounting of guns at his post."

William Heath, from whose memoirs we learn much about the military movements in Westchester County during the following years, came of an old family in Roxbury, Mass. February 9, 1775, he was appointed a general officer by the Congress. Three days after the evacuation of Boston, on March 10, 1776, he left for New York, reaching the city ten days later, and soon after was inoculated with smallpox, and spent a month on Montresor's (now Randall's) Island, "where he went through the operation of that distemper."[92]

On Tuesday, August 27, 1776, the battle of Long Island was fought, the detailed story of which British victory need not here be recited.[93] It was followed two days later by General Washington's masterly withdrawal of his troops across the East River to New York.[94] For the purpose, General Heath had sent him all the boats he could spare from Fort Washington and King's Bridge on the day before.[95] The evacuation of Long Island was at once followed by that of Governor's Island.[96]

For some weeks, then, the British army remained inactive, while the Americans were busy strengthening their fortifications at the northern end of Manhattan Island. Troops reconnoitered the Westchester shore of the Sound to the eastward of Morrisania (Mott Haven), watching the movements of the British on that water. Others were massed in Fort Washington. The works along the East River and at Horn's Hook were strengthened.[97] Reinforcements were asked of the New York Convention for King's Bridge, and a week later some Maryland troops were sent there—barracks had been hastily built—to join the brigades of Generals Mifflin and George Clinton, already stationed at King's Bridge.[98] The brigades of Generals Parsons, Scott, Clinton, Fellows, and G. S. Silliman (of Connecticut, father of Professor Benjamin Silliman of Yale College) had been assigned to duty in New York after the battle of Long Island.[99]

Colonel Putnam examined the position of the Americans and reported them to General Washington on September 3, 1776, as scattered from New York to King's Bridge. He did not think the English could be prevented from landing in New York.[100] General Heath, however, thought the American works both numerous and strong.[101] Graydon, in his Diary, sides with Colonel Putnam, and even bets a beaver hat that no attempt will be made to defend New York.[102]

On September 8, 1776, General Washington issued orders to strengthen the works about King's Bridge, and stationed 9,000 men at the northern end of the island, 5,000 in the city, and the rest of the army between those two points. He evidently

still believed a stand might be made against the enemies'
advance, and relied on the strength of the works from Fort
Washington to King's Bridge and the possibility of obstruct-
ing the Hudson River.[99] These plans General Washington
had no doubt perfected while dining a few days before with
General Heath at the latter's quarters at King's Bridge,[100]
for General Heath leaned strongly to defending the city at any
cost.[101]

The British slowly made preparations to invest the city.
On the day of the battle of Long Island they had sent two
ships into Long Island Sound, and, anchoring off Throg's
Neck (often misnamed Frog's Neck) had reconnoitered the
neighborhood, and, as was their custom, helped themselves to
any cattle they found.[102] Immediately upon General Washington's retreat from Long Island they pushed up the East
River, and were seen in large numbers at the mouth of the
Harlem River.[103] Two of their men-of-war were discovered
on September 2, 1776, at anchor between "Throg's Point"
and the New City (City Island), their crews, as usual, pillag-
ing on shore.[104] A week later they came to closer quarters,
and, after reconnoitering the waters about Hell Gate, they
bombarded the American redoubts at Horen's Hook from their
works on Long Island.[105]

Finally, the British, on September 11, 1776, effected a landing on Montresor's (now Randall's) Island, also on Buchanan's
(now Ward's) Island,[106] and on the Two Brothers' Islands in
sight of the American troops on the Morrisania shore, ordered
there to prevent the British landing on the main land.[107] In
the words of a contemporary chronicler, "Tusday September
ye 10th to Day the Regulars Landed about 6,000 on one of the
Islands Caled the two Brothers."[108] Washington at once
reported this movement to the Congress, and suggested that
nothing could now prevent the enemy's landing in Harlem or
on the main land and attacking him in the rear of the King's
Bridge works.[109] He decided in a council of war, held on
September 12, to evacuate the city and escape with his army
to the north.[110] The valuable stores in the city had already
been removed on September 10.[111]

"Thirsday September ye 12th . . . . orders for all the sick
to move out to King's Bridg Likewise all the Tems Employed

in giting our war-like Stors out of Town."""" On September 14 the stores were sent up by the Bloomingdale and King's Bridge Roads to King's Bridge, and on the next day about eight o'clock "the Brigades in giurel ware ordered to retreat out of town."""" The main body marched toward Fort Washington and King's Bridge ; a rear guard of 4,000 followed, Washington establishing his headquarters at Colonel Roger Morris's (later the Jumel) house.""

This general retreat of the Americans to the northern part of Manhattan Island was made necessary by the British forces landing on the island and threatening to surround the Americans in the southern end. As was expected, the British concentrated their forces on the East River, and about noon on the 15th of September they easily effected a landing with five shiploads of 4,000 men at Turtle and Kepp's Bay (34th Street and East River), some three miles north of the city,"" the Americans hastily abandoning their works in that neighborhood and retreating to the north of the island, a few even crossing into New Jersey."" It is said General Putnam's troops escaped northward from the city, while the British officers were being refreshed at Mrs. Robert Murray's house (on Murray Hill)."" After landing, the British drew up their lines across the island between Horen's Hook (near 89th Street and East River) and Bloomingdale, facing northward."" General Howe established his headquarters in Mr. Apthorpe's house"" (91st Street and 9th Avenue), later a resort known as "Elm Park," and recently moved to the site of Fort George, opposite Fort Number Eight. Outposts were stationed on the heights from MacGowan's Pass along what is now Morningside Heights to the present site of Columbia University, and that of the Clairmont Hotel and General Grant's tomb. Near MacGowan's Pass in and about the stone blockhouse still standing in Central Park, Count Donop and his German troops were stationed. The British army under General Earl Cornwallis lay in the rear.""

On the following day, Monday, September 16, 1776, a little before noon occurred a skirmish between a party of Hessian Jägers, British Light Infantry and Highlanders on the one, and some American riflemen and others on the other side. The result was not decisive, at least the British did not

carry the American position."[128]   In How's Diary we read:[129]
" Some part of our army had a Smart fight with the enimy in
Harlem woods." The site of this so-called " battle of Harlem "
has been confused by a commemorative tablet having been
placed on the walls of Trinity Cemetery, a mile and more from
the actual scene of the engagement.

The British troops were stationed as described above : the
Americans, chiefly some Connecticut light troops, known as
the " Rangers," under Lieutenant Colonel Thomas Knowlton
(who fell in the engagement), and Colonel Weeden's Virginia
regiment, were stationed on the southern slope of the rising
ground north of Manhattanville, or to be exact at about 130th
Street and the Boulevard (a few steps from the present St.
Mary's Church).[130]   The battle began by the above American troops attacking the British flanks opposite them near
General Grant's tomb, Washington directing their movements
from his position in the grounds of the present Sacred Heart
Convent (at one time the residence of Mr. Jacob Lorillard's
family).[131]   The Americans drove the enemy back through
the fields toward their main body. A stubborn resistance was
offered by them in a buckwheat field on the present site of
Columbia University, near what was later the residence of
Mr. Caspar Meier. Finally, reinforcements, chiefly Hessian,
were hurriedly summoned, and the Americans retired to their
former position back of the present St. Mary's Church.[132]

The success of the Americans in this skirmish at Bloomingdale strengthened their belief that the works at the northern
end of Manhattan Island could withstand the British, and, on
the part of the latter, it convinced them that, in preference to
a direct assault upon those scattered works from the south,
which might have been repulsed,[133] a flank movement by
way of Long Island Sound and Westchester County would be
more feasible and less costly. This movement was, as we
shall see, carried out a little less than four weeks later.

This delay afforded the Americans time to still further
fortify themselves on the heights north of Manhattanville and
at Fort Washington,[134] and on the strong grounds about
King's Bridge,[135] where they hoped to fix their winter quarters, unmolested by the enemy.[136]   There they had collected
the public stores.[137]   While the British lay encamped between

the city and the American army,[130] the latter threw up two
lines of intrenchments across the island south of Colonel
Roger Morris's (later the Jumel) house.

It was feared the British would at once attempt to invest
the island, or else land at Morrisania (Mott Haven) or at
Hunt's or Throg's Point and outflank the Americans. To
guard against both these movements, 10,000 men were left at
and near Fort Washington, consisting of Parson's, Scott's and
Dudley Sargent's brigades; Heath's division was increased to
10,000 at King's Bridge, and a floating bridge was thrown
across the Harlem River, as he had suggested, to facilitate
communication between these two bodies, while General
Greene was put in command of the 5,000 troops on the New
Jersey side of the Hudson River.[131] Four hundred and fifty
of Heath's men were also sent from King's Bridge to Morrisania (now Mott Haven), and established a chain of sentinels
along the shore to watch the British on Montresor's (Randall's) Island. The distance separating them was not great,
and General Heath has preserved an amusing account in his
Memoirs of the conversation carried on between the American and English officers.[132] Further east along the shore of
the Sound, near Throg's Neck, Colonel Glover was watching
the movement of the British ships with a view to opposing
the landing of troops.[133]

On September 20, 1776, General Washington rode to King's
Bridge, and inspected the works there. He found them garrisoned with 8,771 men, of whom 1,294 were reported present
sick, and 1,108 as absent sick.[134] Since the battle of Long
Island there had been constant desertions[135]—which, however, were common enough at all times.[136] As King's and
Dykeman's Bridges were the only ones connecting the island
with the main land, a sentinel was stationed there to intercept
deserters, especially those carrying ammunition.[137] One
was stopped, as Graydon tells us,[138] carrying a cannon ball
to his mother with which to pound mustard seed. Sentinels
were also posted for a similar purpose at the Harlem ferry
leading to Morrisania.[139]

On September 21, 1776, occurred a great fire in New York,
destroying Trinity Church among other buildings, which,
with no show of reason, was claimed to have been started by
rebel incendiaries.[140]

On the following day, Sunday, an attempt was made by the Americans to drive the English from Montresor's (Randall's) Island at the mouth of the Harlem River. Two hundred and forty men fell down the river with the tide from King's Bridge in boats, and attempted to land on the island, but were repulsed with the loss of fourteen men. The affair was badly managed, and, in consequence, one captain was cashiered.[146] While this affair was going on, Sunday services were not being neglected in the camp, and How records the text his chaplain preached on, namely Ecclesiastes, viii, 5.[147] A fortnight later the chaplain of Nash's "rigerment" preached from "Luke ye 12 chap 4th & 5th Varses."[148]

On October 3, 1776, a council of war was held under General Heath, and several new redoubts were planned, among them, possibly, the one known later as "King's Battery" (or Redoubt) still standing on the place of Mrs. N. P. Bailey, and one on the east bank of the Harlem River near Morrisania (Mott Haven).[149] Twenty-five men, under Captain Hand, were also assigned to holding the causeway leading to Throg's Point, near a tide-mill, in case the British attempted to land there, which they did, as we shall see.[150]

A few days later, on October 6, 1776, the British were heard embarking at Blackwell's Island and Montresor's (Randall's) Island and moving eastward into Long Island Sound.[151] On October 11th and 12th they landed on Throg's Point (or Neck), on the present site of Fort Schuyler, that point being selected by the advice of their naval officers, who had been taking soundings and found the waters about Pell's Point too shallow.[152] The troops were sent in flat-bottomed boats through Hell Gate.[153] Lord Percy with two brigades of British and one of Hessian soldiers remained in New York, but kept up his connection with General Howe by means of men-of-war posted along the Sound.[154]

This move of General Howe's to Throg's Neck was a brilliant stroke. By gaining the rear of the American army he hoped to cut off its supplies and reënforcements from the east, and thereby either compel Washington to evacuate New York Island or to draw him into a pitched battle in the favorable country of Westchester County.[155]

General Howe remained encamped at Throg's Neck till

October 18, awaiting the arrival of supplies from New York, and also of three battalions of Hessians from Staten Island. For this delay he was severely blamed, it being held that he should have at once moved inland and cut off the Americans' retreat from King's Bridge.[156]

During this time the Americans had been active. The small detachment under Captain Hand stationed on the causeway at Throg's Neck saw the eighty to ninety British boats sail up and land their crews on the point, and succeeded in preventing any general movement inland by the English,[157] or, as Nash has it in his Diary,[158] "Our men ware too much for them they Could not march out from under the covering of their Shiping." How writes in his diary on October 12 :[159] "we were all a larmed and marchd Down Almost there (to Throg's Neck), and Staid All Day the Enemy did not offer any Distance from there Ships."

The garrison about King's Bridge was being constantly reinforced, "and now became the largest part of the American army."[160] McDougal's brigade joined Heath's forces there on October 12, and Wadsworth's and Fellows' brigades followed a few days later.[161] General Heath constantly reconnoitered the Westchester shore, and attempted to extend his left flank so as to prevent any advance by the English from Throg's Neck.[162]

On October 18, 1776, a cloudy and windy day, General Howe, possibly because of the annoyance of the American troops advantageously posted on the causeway, reëmbarked his troops and landed with them at Pell's Point (or Rodman's Neck) to the east of Throg's neck, and near the present City Island, which Stedman, the Tory historian of the Revolution, thinks he should have done at first. He advanced the same day to New Rochelle, driving back the American regiments that opposed him near Pelham Manor.[163] General Heath had dispatched a fresh brigade from King's Bridge to Throg's Neck for that purpose.[164]

The British army was now firmly established in Westchester County, threatening to attack the American army lying in the northern part of New York Island and about King's Bridge in the rear, and thus made its evacuation or eventual capture inevitable.[165] The British had also established themselves in New Jersey by taking Paulus Hook (Jersey City) on the night of September 23.[104]

At first General Washington leaned to evacuating Manhattan Island. General Charles Lee, who had been absent from the previous councils of war, sided with him, and at the council of war held on October 16 urged the necessity of abandoning it. General Greene, however, was opposed. It was finally decided by all, General George Clinton, however, dissenting, to remove all the troops except those in and about Fort Washington and King's Bridge.[105] General Lee, after the capture of Fort Washington, prided himself on having urged its evacuation ; he wrote to Benjamin Rush on November 20, 1776, in a way characteristic of him :[106] "I foresaw, predicted, all that has happened and urged the necessity of abandoning it," and on November 22 he wrote to the Massachusetts Council :[107] "'Twas indecision in our military councils which cost us the garrison of Fort Washington." Others, for instance General Reed, went further in writing[108] " in the affair of Fort Washington, Genl W. manifested an Indecision of Mind which if uncorrected would shade the brighter Parts of his Character."

In compliance with the decision of the council of war, division orders were issued on October 17, 1776, stationing General Heath and General Parsons in Fort Independence with one regiment, General Scott in a redoubt on Cannon Hill, and General Clinton in Valentine's cornfield (presumably on Valentine's Hill) and to the left with three 3-pounders, one 6-pounder and one howitzer.[109] Eleven companies of a regiment of artillery and one colony company were stationed at King's Bridge under Colonel Henry Clay, a total of five hundred and seventy-seven men (including one chaplain and twenty-two drums and fifes).[110] A strong garrison was also left at Fort Washington.[111] The main body of the American army had already begun to move northward on October 12, 1776, along the right bank of the Bronx River, entrenching itself in detached redoubts along the heights from near Woodlawn Cemetery to White Plains, where a fortified camp was established.[112] This movement of the Americans continued for ten days, General Washington following with the rear guard, spending the night of the 21st of October in General Lincoln's headquarters on " Volentine's Hill."[113]

Leaving a strong garrison in and about Fort Washington and a regiment in Fort Independence has fairly been considered a grave error on the part of General Washington. It was leaving those troops to sure capture, as relief or reinforcement was out of the question.'"

Colonel Lasher, who was left in command of Fort Independence, seeing his desperate position—King's Bridge had been evacuated and the barracks burnt by the American army as it marched northward, and his small garrison was growing weak and sickly,'"'—sent to General Heath at White Plains to know what to do, and was ordered by General Washington to destroy the barracks at his fort and to join Colonel Magaw, who had been left in command of the 3,000 men in and about Fort Washington.'"' Colonel Lasher carried out this order on October 27, and hastily evacuated Fort Independence the next day, abandoning the cannon and three hundred stand of small arms.'"" It was high time, for on the following day the enemy appeared from the east, and occupied what was left of the fort.'"°

But to return to the English army at New Rochelle. On October 21 General Howe moved the right center of his line north of the village about two miles on the road toward White Plains.'' On the next day they pushed still further, the "Queen's Rangers" under Colonel Rogers advancing as far as "Marinack" (Mamaroneck), which, in the words of a contemporary, "our militia abandoned with the utmost precipitation—as usual.'"'' On October 24 the British began the march to White Plains, meeting with little resistance.'"' While the British troops were marching northward along the left bank of the Bronx River, the American army was proceeding in the same direction along the right bank, breaking up their detached camps on the heights from Valentine's Hill to White Plains (described above) as they marched northward.'"' These two hostile columns marching parallel through Westchester County committed depredations on the farms, which became a common occurrence and the cause of much suffering to the inhabitants from then on till 1783 and the end of the war.'"°

On Sunday and Monday, October 27 and 28, 1776, the two armies met in battle at White Plains,'"" the cannonading

being heard as far off as at Fort Washington. The result was
not decisive, but certainly not favorable to General Washington, who on October 31 with rare skill withdrew his army
northward five miles to the broken country about North
Castle, where General Howe did not care to follow him.[97]
In fact, as one English authority has it:[98] "they were, as
usual, too expeditious for our pursuit." This epitomizes
General Washington's skill as a general. His military success
and the successes of the other American leaders was largely
due to their ability to run away from the English troops and
to escape being drawn into battle except under circumstances
most favorable to their side. Witness the battles of Saratoga
and Yorktown.

The English army in America was perhaps the best equipped,
organized and officered military body ever seen up to that
time, and, as we know, found no difficulty in occupying the
leading cities along the coast and overrunning the neighboring
districts ; but the nature of the country, the poor means of
transportation and provisioning an army in the interior made
it impossible for them to subjugate and hold more than a narrow strip along tide water. We won our independence by
wearing out the British as much as by the military and finan-
cial help France gave us.

The strength of Howe's army was partly due to the large
contingent of German troops, the use of which the German
princes had, with questionable morality, rented to the English
government. These Germans made excellent soldiers. To be
sure, they are said to have got drunk regularly on their
monthly pay-day,[99] but that was a weakness prevalent at
the time in the best families, and, no doubt, the Americans
would have acted similarly if they had been lucky enough to
have a regular pay-day.

The Hessian uniform must have been quite imposing : a
towering brass-fronted cap ; moustaches dyed black with shoe-
polish, hair plastered with tallow and flour, a cue hanging to
the waist ; a blue coat almost covered with broad belts sup-
porting the cartouche box, a brass-hilted sword and bayonet,
a yellow waist-coat with flaps, yellow breeches, and black
gaiters up to the knees.[100] The German officers were a well-
educated lot, and proficient in the art of war. General Knyp-

hausen, who we shall see distinguished himself in the capture of Fort Washington, was about sixty-six years old, a fine looking German about five feet eleven inches tall, straight and slender.[91] His features were sharp, and his appearance martial. He was a native of Alsace, and followed his father's calling, who had served in the army of Frederick William I of Prussia, the father of Frederick the Great. After a distinguished career in America he returned to Germany in 1782, and was succeeded by Lieutenant General Lossberg.[92]

The first batch of Hessian troops started from their home on February 29, 1776 ; among them were Ditfurth's, Donop's, Knyphausen's and Rall's battalions. On March 10 they marched through Bremen, and a week later set sail for England. Some of them reached Sandy Hook on August 17. Another batch marched to Bremen from Cassel and set sail on March 22.[93] Some Hessians took part in the battle of Long Island on August 27,[94] and were with the English soldiers when they landed on Manhattan Island on September 15, and joined them in the lines north of the city, e. g. Donop's battalion.

The second division of Hessians under Lieutenant General Knyphausen arrived in New York harbor on October 18, 1776, together with a regiment of Waldeck troops, six hundred and seventy strong.[95] These were at once dispatched in many flat-bottomed boats up the East River into the Sound, described as a beautiful sight on a fine day (October 22) by a contemporary newspaper reporter. There they joined the English troops which had already advanced beyond New Rochelle.[96] General Knyphausen lay with his troops near the village of New Rochelle for nearly a week, while the English troops were pressing on to White Plains and engaging the Americans there.

On October 28, the day of the battle of White Plains, General Knyphausen was ordered by General Howe to leave the Waldeck regiment at New Rochelle, and to move with his six battalions of Hessians to King's Bridge. This he did, and took post at Mile Square and Valentine's Hill.[97] On November 2 he continued his march to King's Bridge, and, crossing Dykeman's Bridge, encamped on the northern end of Manhattan Island opposite Spuyten Duyvil, the Americans retiring before his advance to the shelter of Fort Washington, the barracks about King's Bridge, it will be remembered, having been burned and the works abandoned a few days before by Colonel Lasher's men.[198]

The Waldeck regiment followed Knyphausen, and established itself on November 4 in the ruins of Fort Independence.[199] General Grant on that day marched with the fourth brigade to Mile Square and Valentine's Hill. The sixth brigade also marched to the neighborhood of DeLancey's Mills (Bronxdale).[200]

The main army under General Howe at White Plains also joined these forces for the purpose of investing Fort Washington and the entire island of New York. Leaving the American army to itself in North Castle, General Howe retired from White Plains on November 4, and, marching towards the Hudson River, encamped at Dobbs Ferry two days later, where supplies could easily reach him from New York by water.[201] This apparently sudden change of plan on Howe's part is most easily explained by supposing that he found it impossible to draw Washington into a general engagement, and preferred to retire and secure New York, where convenient winter quarters could be established.[202] Stedman says:[203] "Convinced that it was part of the enemy's system studiously to avoid an action and that their knowledge of the country enabled them to execute this system with an advantage, General Howe resolved to cease an ineffectual pursuit and employ himself in the reduction of King's Bridge and Fort Washington."

Some thought wrongly at the time that Howe was retreating before Washington.[204] General Heath and General Greene (at Fort Lee) entertained some such notion,[205] and even one of the English generals four years later said:[206] "The rebels whom we had not thought worth pursuing, now pursued us and ravished the Chester counties." A clergyman in Greenwich, Connecticut, preaching a historical sermon a year later, uses these words:[207] "The enemy crossed in their expectations (at White Plains) now despaired of compassing their design, gave over the pursuit and returned with shame."

Some, however, saw the real meaning of the British movement, and none more clearly than General Washington himself, who, on November 6, reports the unexpected advance toward the Hudson River and King's Bridge to Congress, and expresses his fears that Fort Washington is to be attacked. He expresses the same fear in a letter to Governor Livingston on the following day.[207] General Greene, too, early saw the real meaning of the British movement.[208]

On November 7, some artillery joined General Knyphausen at King's Bridge under a strong escort, also four battalions of Light Infantry, the remainder of the Chasseurs, and four field pieces. General Greene reports to General Washington from Fort Lee that 1,500 British have taken possession of the slope north of "Spiten Devil," but thinks they cannot penetrate any further.[210] The British and Hessians were reconnoitering the approaches to Fort Washington on the same day. The Americans could distinctly see them on the plains south of King's Bridge. The Hessians could also be seen throwing up intrenchments in that neighborhood.[211] On November 8 and 9 these Hessians received a drubbing at the hands of a scouting party from the 3d and 5th Pennsylvania battalions stationed at Fort Washington.[212]

In the meantime the main body of the English lay encamped at Dobbs Ferry, but on November 12, a "varry raw cold day," they broke camp at nine a. m., and marched in two columns to Phillipsburg (Yonkers), and pitched their tents near Phillips' manor (still standing and used as a court-house).[213] Next day they moved on, and encamped on the "heights of Fordham . . . forming a line with the right to the Brunx, upon the Westchester Road, and the left to the North River."[214] The British army was now ready to begin active preparations to invest Fort Washington. A brigade of Hessians had been added to Knyphausen's forces at King's Bridge.[215] Thirty flat-boats had also been sent up the North River on the night of November 14, under Captains Wilkinson and Molloy, without being observed from Fort Washington, and were taken through Spuyten Duyvil Creek to the Harlem River and King's Bridge.[216]

To assist in the coming attack on Fort Washington, a redoubt, called "Number Eight," had been hastily built on the site of the present house of Mrs. Gustav Schwab, and armed with some heavy artillery transported there (presumably

from New York), and also some field pieces."[1] Graydon
quotes a friend's description of this redoubt:[2] "On the
west side of Haerlem River (on Laurel Hill), a body of men
was posted to watch the motions of the enemy, who had erected
works on the high and commanding ground east of that river,
apparently with the design of covering a landing of the troops
in that part of the island of New York."

This important redoubt was finished on November 15,[3]
and in the afternoon of that day General Howe sent Lieutenant Colonel Patterson to Fort Washington to demand its
surrender of Colonel Magaw, the commander, which he
refused.[4]

The situation, then, on the eve of the battle, was as follows:
Knyphausen's Hessians and the Waldeck regiment were
encamped near King's Bridge under Köhlen, Stein, Witgenau,
Wissenbach, Huyne, Bienau, Rall and Lossberg. A battery
of Hessian artillery was stationed in the flat land, east of the
site of the present Inwood school house.[5] These forces
were to storm the American works from the north. On the
east of the Harlem River was Fort Number Eight, which was
to assist the First and Second battalions of Light Infantry and
two battalions of Guards under General Mathews, and a
reserve consisting of the First and Second Grenadiers with the
Thirty-third Regiment under Lord Cornwallis, in landing on
the opposite shore and storming the redoubts on Laurel Hill.
General Mathews' forces had been sent to the neighborhood of
Fort Number Eight by way of the Hudson, Spuyten Duyvil
Creek and Harlem River in the above-mentioned boats.[6]
Further south the American works along the west bank of the
Harlem were to be carried by the Forty-second Regiment
under Colonel Sterling. They were to cross the river about
opposite the Roger Morris house.[7] From the south Lord
Percy with his English and Hessian columns was to carry the
two lines of intrenchments across the island and press on to
Fort Washington.[8] The English man-of-war "Pearl," which
conveyed General Howe to this country, was also stationed in
the Hudson River, one mile north of Jeffrey's Hook, to assist
in the attack and prevent the escape of the garrison.[9]

Opposed to these British forces were the American garrisons
at Fort Washington and the outlying redoubts, in all about

3,000 men. Of these 1,200 formed the garrison of Fort Washington itself, of whom two hundred to three hundred had been sent as a reinforcement from Colonel Durkee's regiment by General Greene from Fort Lee on October 21.[384] The troops in the fort were chiefly from Pennsylvania and Maryland, and belonged to the Third, Fifth and <u>Sixth</u> Pennsylvania battalions.[387] Of the Fifth battalion two hundred and two were reported present and fit for duty on November 15, and three absent without leave. Two weeks before the battalion had been twice as large.[388]

These troops in Fort Washington were under the command of Colonel Robert Magaw, who had been left there on Washington's retiring with his army to White Plains.[389] This brave officer, a lawyer by profession, hailed from Pennsylvania. He had been made a colonel by the Congress early in 1776; soon after he was put in command of the Sixth Pennsylvania regiment (or battalion). He was made a prisoner in the capture of Fort Washington, remained in prison four years, was finally exchanged in 1780, and retired from the army. He died in Carlisle, Pennsylvania, in December, 1789, and is buried there in the Meeting House Cemetery.[390]

At the end of the same ridge with and north of Fort Washington, and overlooking Inwood, the redoubt which had been built was manned with a small garrison of two hundred and ninety-seven men, mostly from Fort Lee, the rest Maryland militia men, under the command of Colonel Rawlins.[391] The redoubt on Cock Hill overlooking Spuyten Duyvil Creek had presumably been abandoned by the Americans on the approach of the Hessians a fortnight before.

Another outpost of Fort Washington was the one on Laurel Hill (later called "Fort George"), a commanding position which was manned by some Pennsylvania militia under Colonel Baxter of Bucks County, Pennsylvania.[392] To the south Colonel Cadwallader's forces manned the intrenchments which commanded the approach from that direction.[393]

From this description of the relative disposition of the American and British troops it is seen how hopeless the contest necessarily was, and General Washington, as he took in the situation from his point of observation on the Palisades near Fort Lee—he had moved his army into New Jersey from

North Castle in the meantime, arriving at General Greene's quarters at Fort Lee on November 13,—must have felt a keen regret at having allowed himself to be persuaded by General Greene to leave a garrison in the forts opposite and sacrifice them to certain capture.[231] As late as November 8 he still hesitated to leave the garrison in Fort Washington owing to the ineffective obstructions in the Hudson River.[232] These he had been attempting since June to construct between Forts Washington and Lee, but to no purpose, for the English ships invariably broke them.[233] Those ordered on September 8, 1776, were easily passed on the morning of October 9, by three English ships and their tenders, which "came up the North river By fort Wors'n and run up about fifteen miles and anchored." There they sent their crews ashore at Dobbs Ferry to plunder. Nash tells us in his Journal "they took two of our galleys and a Sloop and a schooner Loaded with rum."[234] Two days later Washington had a narrow escape, for, coming down the Hudson in a barge, a shot from one of these English men-of-war killed three of his crew.[235]

Doubtless General Washington's attempt to hold Fort Washington was one of the most serious errors he committed during the Revolution;[236] while Lord Howe's plan of surrounding that fort and the disposition of his troops was a brilliant manœuvre, and has excited the admiration of writers on the war.[237]

The chance discovery of a letter dated some years later adds curiously to our knowledge of Howe's plans. It has always seemed strange that Howe should have been apparently so familiar with the disposition of the American troops about Fort Washington and been able to direct his attacks accordingly. Graydon threw out the following suggestion:[238] "Howe must have had a perfect knowledge of the ground we occupied. This he might have acquired from hundreds in New York; but he might have been more thoroughly informed of everything desirable to be known from one Dement of Magaw's battalion, who was intelligent in points of duty, and deserted to the enemy a week before the assault. This man was probably an emissary from them; he was an European, I recollect, and not originally an officer of the corps; his name, at least, is not among those appointed by the Committee of

Safety." Graydon describes him as "a coarse, ill-looking man."

This suspicion of Graydon's was confirmed in a strange way by the discovery many years after of the following letter of William Demont (or Dement) to Rev. Dr. Peters of the Church of England, dated January 16, 1792 (now in the possession of Mr. E. F. DeLancey):[12]

"Revd Sir

Permit me to trouble you with a Short recital of my Services in America which I Presume may be Deem'd among the Most Singular of any that will go to upper Canada (he wanted a claim on the English officials in Canada). On the 2d of Novr 1776 I Sacrificed all I was worth in the world to the Service of my King & Country & Joined the then Lord Percy brought in with (me) the Plans of Fort Washington by which Plans that Fortress was taken by his Majesty's Troops the 16 instant. . . . these Sir are facts well known to every General Officer which was there—and I may with Truth Declare from the time I studied the Interest of my Country & Neglected my own—or in the Language of Cardinal Woolsey had I served my God as I have done my king he would not Thus have Forsaken me."

He then offers a bill for his services[13] "for engaging Guides, getting intelligence &c. 45£. 9s. 9d. For doing duty as commissary of Prisoners at Philadelphia etc. 26£. 13s. 8d."

This remarkable confession is borne out by a closer examination of the contemporary sources, and is accepted by such authorities as Professor H. P. Johnston, Mrs. M. J. Lamb and J. G. Wilson.[14] It seems this William Demont (or Dement) had entered Magaw's battalion in Philadelphia as ensign, by the appointment of the Pennsylvania Council of Safety, on January 1, 1776,[15] Graydon's statement notwithstanding. On February 29, 1776, this Council or Committee appointed him Adjutant to the Fifth Pennsylvania battalion, which position he continued to hold while it was stationed at Fort Washington, where he signed the returns for his battalion, for instance on October 7, 1776.[16] His desertion on November 2 is corroborated by his appearing on the rolls as "absent without leave" on that day.[17] Doubtless he carried the plans of the fort and its outposts, with much additional information, to Lord Percy, who, it will be remembered, had been left on

Manhattan Island near Harlem, when Lord Howe moved with his troops to Throg's Neck and White Plains."[157]

Even granted that Demont or his papers were at once sent to the commander-in-chief, Lord Howe, at White Plains, it is extremely doubtful whether the receipt of the information caused him to suddenly change his plans, withdraw from facing Washington and hasten southward to invest New York, as Mr. E. F. DeLancey and others would have us believe."[148]

Such an explanation assumes that Demont deserted, communicated with Lord Percy, reached the British army at White Plains, and that the latter broke camp and started for Dobbs' Ferry—all in two days. It also overlooks the important fact that five days before Demont's desertion General Knyphausen had been ordered by General Howe to march from New Rochelle to King's Bridge, and that he reached that place with his Hessians on the day Demont communicated with the English. The relation of these dates ought to leave it beyond question that "although the British commander must have intended to attack Fort Washington, he was doubtless confirmed in his intentions by (the) information received." [149]

An order of General Howe's, dated October 5, 1777, putting this "Captain Dement, Fourier de la Cour," in charge of the Rebel Prisoners as Commissary of Prisoners, confirms another item in the deserter's confession.[151] However, his claim that every English general officer knew of his feat cannot be verified. Presumably he, like the above historians, exaggerated the importance of his achievement. Certainly no American officer, except Graydon as mentioned above, knew or suspected his treachery, which, in evil intention at least, rivalled that of Benedict Arnold four years later.[152]

ATTACK ON FORT WASHINGTON.[249]

On Saturday, November 16, 1776, the famous attack on Fort Washington was made from the four directions indicated above. The battle began early in the morning with a cannonade on the part of the Hession battery on the plain near the Century House directed at Colonel Rawlins' position on the heights south of Inwood.[254] The batteries at Fort Number Eight and those further down the Harlem River joined in this bombardment,[255] directing their fire at Baxter's redoubt on Laurel Hill and at Cadwallader's position near the Roger Morris (the Jumel) house. Graydon, who was himself stationed on the southern lines opposing Lord Percy's advance, describes[256] the "tremendous roar of artillery, quickly succeeded by incessant vollies of small arms, which seemed to proceed from the east and north." [257]

In fact, the main and most stubborn attack was made from the north about noon by the Hessians advancing from King's Bridge.[258] In the words of General Heath :[259] "General Knyphausen, with a heavy column of Hessians, advanced by King's Bridge. They were discovered by the Americans from the high ground north of Fort Washington, as day broke, and cannonaded from the field pieces at this advanced post. The Hessian column divided into two ; the right ascending the strong broken ground towards Spitten-Devil Creek ; the left nearer the road, towards the gorge. The first obtained the ground without much difficulty, but the Americans made a most noble opposition against the latter and for a considerable time kept them from ascending the hill, making a terrible slaughter among them ; but the great superiority of the assailants, with an unabating firmness, finally prevailed ; their loss was greater here than any other place."

This is, perhaps, the best contemporary description of the advance of the Hessian and Waldeck troops upon Fort Washington. Bancroft's description is more picturesque but probably imaginary :[260] "Excited by the obstinacy of the contest, Rall (the commander of the Hessian right wing) cried out 'Forward, my Grenadiers, every man of you,' his drums beat, his trumpets blew the notes of command, and all who

escaped the fire from behind rocks and trees shouted ' Hurrah '
and pushed forward without firing.''

General Knyphausen's orders for the attack have been preserved.[201] The Jägers and forty Grenadiers under Captain
Bornin were to act as skirmishers ; one hundred and sixty
men under Colonel Borbeck were to follow. Then were to
come the Grenadiers under Köhler and those of Wutgenau
(Witgenau), Lossberg, Rall, Knyphausen, Huyne, Bünau and
the Waldeck regiment. Orders for the assault were given in
detail. The advance was to begin at 5.30 a. m. Colonel Rall
commanded the right wing, with Donop commanding the
skirmish line, which advanced along the heights overlooking
the Hudson River from Spuyten Duyvil Creek, with difficulty
crowding back Colonel Rawlins' brave Maryland troops
toward Fort Washington,[202] where he was joined by General
Knyphausen, who had advanced with the left wing along the
King's Bridge Road, and forced his way through the woods to
within gunshot of Fort Washington.[203]

The garrison in Fort Number Eight could plainly see the
Hessians advancing on Fort Washington from the north, and
assisted the movement by vigorously bombarding Colonel
Baxter's position opposite.[204] To assist still further in the
attack from the north, General Mathews, who had been lying
with his Second battalion of Guards and his First and Second
battalions of Light Infantry under the protection of the guns
of Fort Number Eight, advanced to the river's edge, and,
crossing in thirty boats to the opposite shore, he landed his
troops in Sherman's Creek and immediately advanced with
them up the steep slope of Laurel Hill. General Lord Cornwallis immediately followed with his two battalions of Grenadiers as well as the Thirty-third regiment (the latter had
been sent as a reinforcement from King's Bridge). Headed
by the light infantry, this body stormed the redoubts on
Laurel Hill, but were at first much harassed by the American
riflemen hidden behind stones and trees.[205]

The following is Graydon's description :[206] " The militia
under Colonel Baxter, posted on Harlem River (Laurel Hill)
were attacked by the British guards and light infantry, who
landed on the island of New York, protected by the fire from
the work on the heights, on the opposite side of the river

(Fort Number Eight). A short contest ensued, but our troops, overpowered by numbers, and leaving behind them Colonel Baxter, who was killed by a British officer as he was bravely encouraging his men, retired to the fort (Fort Washington)."

General Heath describes the attack in less detail.[361] General Howe's description is also meagre.[362] Lossing says :[363] "General Mathews pushed up the wooded heights, drove Baxter's troops from their redoubt (Laurel Hill) and rocky defence and stood victors upon the hills overlooking the open fields around Fort Washington."

Carrington is no more circumstantial :[370] "The division of Mathews and Cornwallis, which had been in readiness, landed, although under heavy fire, pushed back the resisting force, and moved over Laurel Hill to take the works (Fort Washington) in the center."

DeLancey describes the attack as follows :[371] "Just as the Germans became fully engaged the British regiments of light infantry and guards, four in number, under Brigadier General Mathews, supported by the First and Second Grenadiers and the Thirty-third Foot, under Cornwallis, in thirty boats under cover of a tremendous fire from the British batteries on its Westchester side, crossed Harlem River to Sherman's Creek. Though met with a sharp fire, they instantly ascended the face of Laurel Hill, high, wooded and precipitous, the falling leaves, yet moist with the rain of the preceding day, rendering the footing still more difficult and drove from the battery on its brows and its summit the Pennsylvania troops (the last reënforcement sent over from Fort Lee) whom Magaw had detailed to defend it. Though defeated and forced to retreat, they made a brave defense, Colonel Baxter, their commander, being killed, sword in hand, at the head of his men."

Johnson, in his Life of Nathaniel Greene,[372] describes the attack on Laurel Hill as follows : "A strong column of British troops, commanded by some of Howe's best officers, had been held in reserve on the eastern bank of the Harlem, and so completely masked from view, that when the Americans thought themselves engaged with the whole British force, to their astonishment they were apprised that a formidable and fresh enemy was descending the Harlem, and about to effect a

landing on the rocky shore which extends northwardly from
the post occupied by Colonel Baxter. Pressed before by very
superior numbers, this new danger which threatened the rear
of both Rawlins and Cadwallader required immediate attention.
About one hundred and fifty men dispatched from Cadwallader's command, and one hundred from the fort in vain
opposed a prompt and resolute resistance to eight hundred
picked men, already landed and forcing their way up the hill.
But the contest was not bloodless."

An early English history of the war says:"" "The light
infantry landed and were exposed both before and after to a
very brisk and continual fire from the provincials, who were
themselves covered by the rocks and the trees among which
they were posted. The former, however, with their usual
alertness and activity, extricated themselves by clambering
up a very steep and rough mountain, and made way for the
landing of the troops without opposition."

Murray, writing in 1780, says:"" "The second (attack) on
the east was led by Brigadier-General Matthews, at the head
of the First and Second battalions of Light Infantry and Third
battalion of Guards, supported by Lord Cornwallis with the
First and Second battalions of Grenadiers and the Thirty-
third regiment. These troops crossed the East River in flat
boats, and as the enemies' works there extended the breadth of
the island, redoubts and batteries were erected on the opposite
shore, both to cover the landing of the troops, and to annoy
those works which were near the water."

While the British were successfully approaching Fort Washington from the north and northeast, General Sterling had carried the American earthworks overlooking the Harlem near
Colonel Roger Morris's house with his Forty-second High-
lander regiment and two battalions of the Second brigade. He
had crossed the Harlem (at about 160th Street) and stormed
the heights, driving back the small body of Americans who
opposed him, capturing one hundred and seventy of their number. Driving the remainder before him, he rapidly moved
toward Fort Washington."" This movement of General Sterling's had been intended merely as a feint, but he found it an
easy matter to drive back the Americans from their redoubt,
and followed up his advantage by moving directly on Fort
Washington.""

A letter from headquarters, dated November 29, 1776,[177] reads thus; "On Saturday, the 16th inst., about two o'clock afternoon, a Body of British troops from New York, with a body of Hessians from King's Bridge, made an attack upon our Lines at that Place. At the same time a number of Boats from the Shipping Came up Harlem River and landed a Party of them, who advanced forward with an Intention to cut off our Retreat, which in part they effected; But a part of our Men taking advantage of a Hill got safe to the Fort."

The fourth attack upon Fort Washington was made from the south by Lord Percy's leading a corps of British and a column of Hessian troops from Bloomingdale, where they had been encamped, driving back the Americans from their outposts intrenched south of Fort Washington, and approached close to that fort.[178]

As General Washington watched the attack from the Palisades opposite in company with Tom Paine and others,[179] he soon realized the inevitable result, and dispatched Captain Gooch of Boston across the river to urge Colonel Magaw to hold out till evening, when he would attempt to get the garrison into New Jersey. It was too late, however. Captain Gooch, after delivering the message, barely eluded the enemy, who almost surrounded the fort, and reached his boat and the other shore with difficulty.[180]

Cut off from retreat, and open to the bombardment by the British artillery, Colonel Magaw was compelled to surrender the fort about sundown.[181] He has been blamed for doing so, but without reason.[182]

In his report to the Committee of Safety on November 16, 1776, General Washington reported the number of prisoners as about 2,000.[183] In point of fact, there were more. The English report[184] puts the number at 2,586, which must have been nearer the truth. Among them were four colonels, four lieutenant-colonels, five majors, forty-six captains, one hundred and seven lieutenants, thirty-one ensigns, one chaplain, two adjutants, two quartermasters, five surgeons, two commissaries, one engineer, one wagon master. Among the ordnance captured were four 32-pounders, two 18-pounders, seven 12-pounders, five 9-pounders, fifteen 6-pounders, eight 3-pounders, two 5½ inch howitzers, beside the cannon previously captured about King's Bridge.[185]

Graydon has given us an amusing account of his being taken
prisoner ; he was much annoyed by the officers of the light
infantry (who had stormed Laurel Hill), " for the most part
young and insolent puppies."[206]

The attack had cost a good many lives. The Hessians alone
lost fifty-three ; two hundred and seventy-three of them were
wounded.[207] The list of killed and wounded Pennsylvania
officers is preserved.[208]

The report of the capture of Fort Washington traveled
slowly. It reached Philadelphia on November 18, 1776, and
was not credited " but by our enemies and the timorous and
faint-hearted amongst us." Two days later the news was confirmed.[209]

How, who was presumably with the American army in New
Jersey at the time, notes in his diary on November 17,[210] " We
hear that Fort Washington was taken By the Enimy Yester-
day."

The rumor of the capture reached New Haven November
20,[211] which was followed a week later by a full report of the
battle, as usual not correct in its details.[212] Colonel Magaw,
for instance, was misnamed " Genl McGraw."

By December 1, 1776, the news had reached the neighborhood of Boston and had been confirmed.[213]

The capture of Fort Washington was a heavy blow to the
American cause. Not only did it insure to the British the
unmolested possession of New York Island—though, as we
have seen, this was inevitable,—but, above all, it deprived the
American army of a large body of soldiers who were now prisoners of war instead of swelling the dwindling ranks of Washington's army. Their number and names are preserved.[214]
The loss of these men was the more severe, as it was felt that
they had been uselessly sacrificed, and had been left to no purpose in Fort Washington on the withdrawal of the American
army to White Plains.

The British troops were pleased with their success, and even
did some uncalled-for bragging. One English officer writes
ten days later[215] of Fort Washington as "the strongest post
that ever was occupied by an army. . . . . Hannibal, in his
passage over the Alps, could not have met with grounds or
difficulties more formidable than what the Hessians had to go

over." A Tory newspaper of New York of about the same
date says :[294] "the ground and Defences about Fort Washington are so very strong and advantageous, that a correspondent
supposes, a Handful of British Troops would have maintained
the Place for six months against an army of Thirty Thousand
men."

In point of fact, the American garrison could under no con-
ceivable circumstances have withstood the British attack,
which does not seem to have been marked with more than
ordinary courage, considering the odds in favor of the British
troops, well equipped and ably commanded as they were,
attacking a much smaller number of poorly disciplined and
raw American troops.

THE WAR IN WESTCHESTER COUNTY.

After capturing Fort Washington, and thus assuring themselves unmolested control of New York Island, the British
prepared to go into winter quarters. General Greene, writing to General Washington from Fort Lee on November 18,
1776, just before he evacuated that post, reports the movement
of the British troops on the opposite shore of the Hudson
River,[97] and General Lee, writing to General Washington a
few days later, notes the massing of the enemy about King's
Bridge.[98]

Fort Washington was named Fort Knyphausen in honor of
that intrepid commander, to whom its capture was so largely
due, and he was put in command of that post, which he
strengthened and garrisoned with his Hessian troops as an outpost of New York, and a barrier to a possible invasion of the
island from the north.[99]

In fact, it was highly necessary to guard against incursions
by the Americans from the north, and Fort Independence, and
particularly Fort Number Eight, played a prominent part, as
we shall see, in the incessant skirmishes of the following seven
years ; small bands of Americans constantly sweeping down
on those posts from their strongholds in upper Westchester
County, and threatening their capture.[100]

In January, 1777, for instance, at Washington's command,
who hoped thereby to lead the British to withdraw some of
their troops from New Jersey, General Heath, whom General
Lincoln and a body of militia had joined, approached New
York from the north with 4,000 men. On January 17 and 18,
1777, they moved toward King's Bridge ; one column under
Lincoln marching from Tarrytown to the heights above
Colonel Van Courtland's house ; another column of Connecticut troops under Generals Wooster and Parsons approaching from New Rochelle and East Chester, which they had
reached two days before ; and the third column under General
Scott, to which General Heath attached himself, from White
Plains. The last two columns took position on the heights
east of King's Bridge.[101] A British outpost gave the alarm at
the approach of the Americans in the early morning, and the

pickets were at once withdrawn behind the protecting guns of Fort Independence. Heath placed a battery south of the fort on the heights above Dykeman's (now Farmer's) Bridge to bombard the fort and also a body of Hessians which appeared below from King's Bridge, and with good effect, for the Hessians withdrew "as fast as they could without running" behind the redoubt and hill named Fort Prince Charles at King's Bridge (on Marble Hill).[302]

The cannonade of the fort continued three days, but evidently did little damage, for General Heath was obliged to send to North Castle for heavier ordnance on January 22, which arrived five days later, but proved to be useless. In the mean time there were daily skirmishes. A storm came on, and Lincoln's troops, encamped in huts in the woods to the north of the fort, were compelled to retire. The British, too, made repeated and successful sallies, one to DeLancey's Mills (Bronxdale), and one to Valentine's Hill, driving back the Americans from their positions. The latter retaliated by sending a detachment to Morrisania (now Mott Haven) to light fires, which greatly frightened the British garrisons on Montresor's (Randall's) Island and in Fort Washington.[303]

The weather grew worse, a heavy snow storm came on, and on January 29, 1777, the Americans, unable to draw out the British garrison from Fort Independence or Fort Number Eight into skirmishes on terms favorable to them, and being without efficient ordnance, retired in three columns, as they had come, to Tarrytown, White Plains and New Rochelle.[304]

A few days later, Colonel Enos was sent with a detachment of Americans to surprise Fort Independence, with no result, however.[305]

Till late in 1777 there was no skirmishing about New York worth mentioning. But in November of that year a party of Colonel Emerick's Chasseurs from King's Bridge, where they were stationed, moved northward on a marauding expedition. They captured Peter and Cornelius Van Tassel. The Americans retaliated by moving down the Hudson in boats from Tarrytown under Abraham Martlingh. Passing the enemy's water guards, and landing a little below Spuyten Duyvil Creek, they burned the house of General Oliver DeLancey, the leading Tory.[306]

During the summer of 1777 the British garrison in New York and about King's Bridge consisted of the following regiments : The Guards ; the 45th (which at one time was stationed at Fort Number Eight), 35th, 4th, 28th, 49th, 26th, 7th, 63d, 52d, the 1st and 2d battalions of the 71st, Simcoe's Rangers, Emerick's Chasseurs, {the last two corps were largely recruited from American loyalists, and were generally stationed at King's Bridge).[307] Lord Cathcart's Legion (which was stationed at King's Bridge a year later),[308] the Irish Volunteers, Bayard's Corps, a corps attached to the artillery, and the following Hessian regiments : Prince Charles, Tromback, Donop, Mirbach, Knyphausen, Lossberg, Wellart, Seitzt, Wisenbach, Hereditary Prince (Erbprinz), and the Hessian Grenadiers under Linsing, Mingerode, Larquhay and Kuyler. These troops lay quietly in and about New York during the rest of 1777 and the first half of 1778. Insignificant expeditions into the "Neutral Country" were made by the "Queen's Ranger's, in May, 1778, for instance, to Croton Bridge, and later to Mamaroneck.[309]

But in July, 1778, the Americans became bolder, and under General Scott hovered about the English outposts at Forts Independence and Number Eight, moving rapidly through the country between Yonkers and New Rochelle. They frequently sent their patrols to William's Bridge (over the Bronx) and to Valentine's Hill, and kept Emerick's Chasseurs and Simcoe's Rangers in a constant state of alarm.[310] Occasionally the Americans and British would meet in an indecisive skirmish, as on August 20, 1778, when Emerick's corps was attacked.[311] This corps and the Rangers were encamped outside of King's Bridge, and had just been reinforced by some loyalist troops, as "the post was of great extent, liable to insult and required many sentinels."[312]

It was inevitable that the British and American troops should now and then meet, as they roamed through the "Neutral Country" (made famous by Cooper) in lower Westchester County in small detachments on foraging and marauding expeditions. These were of frequent occurrence. Thus, in September, 1778, the 71st regiment of light troops under Colonel Campbell advanced to Mile Square. At the same time the loyalist troops (the "Queen's Rangers," DeLancey's

"Cow-boys," Emerick's corps and some cavalry under Simcoe, also some Hessians under Knyphausen) were scouring the country beyond the Bronx and toward the Chesters.[313]

Not only did the British have to keep a lookout for American troops; the Stockbridge Indians also joined in the fun—they were old hands in such matters,[314]—and had to be repulsed from King's Bridge by Simcoe.[315]

One gets the clearest notion of the conditions in the British garrisons and the life led by the soldiers from the interesting journal kept by Von Krafft, a German soldier in the Hessian brigade, who deserves more than passing notice. J. C. P. Von Krafft was born in Dresden in 1752. Anxious to join in the American war, he volunteered on an American privateer, but, after reaching this country in July, 1778, he joined his countryman Donop's regiment, in which he became a corporal in September, 1781. A year later he rose to a lieutenantcy in von Bose's regiment. While in this country he secretly married Miss Cornelia de la Metre in 1783, and settled here after the war, as many of his countrymen did, first in New York as a teacher, and later in the Capitol as a government employee. His descendants still live in Washington.[316]

Immediately on being enrolled with the Hessians, he marched with them to "Blumendal" (Bloomingdale), and encamped there. Soon he was attached to the garrisons at Fort Knyphausen (Fort Washington) and King's Bridge.[317] One day he was sent with others to guard the powder magazine at "Tortelbey," where he found time to do some successful foraging, for he writes, "never until then did I eat so many cherries and oysters as in this place."[318] As a result, he spent some days in the hospital. Another day he spends in visiting friends in the "Erbprinz" regiment, which was encamped on a hill from which one could see the East River and "King's Pritsch" (evidently the redoubt Fort George on Laurel Hill).[319] Later in July, 1778, he joined the Chasseurs, one hundred and nineteen men, stationed at Colonel Roger Morris's (the Jumel) house, at that time General Knyphausen's headquarters. With them he marched to "Spakent Hill" opposite Fort "Intepentence" (his Saxon origin still influenced his pronunciation and spelling) near the Van Cortlandt house, and encamped there (evidently on the heights north of and over-

looking Spuyten Duyvil Creek). He records that the mosqui-
toes made sleep impossible.[20]

Von Krafft tells us in detail about the foraging expeditions
into Westchester County which he joined. Once they moved
northward to Yonkers, and encamped at the famous Phillips'
manor. Evidently provisions were scarce, and the Hessians
mutinous in consequence.[21] Later he joined an expedition to
"Weit Blene," where he stole his share of pigs, fowl and fruit,
and enjoyed the chestnuts which were then ripe. Toward
the end of the year 1778 his battalion was frequently on patrol
duty. On one of these occasions the Americans attacked their
outposts, who were fast asleep, robbed them of their arms, and
let them go after a sound drubbing. Such skirmishes were
frequent.[23]

In November, 1778, Von Krafft was stationed in the redoubt
overlooking Spuyten Duyvil Creek, and in December, 1778,
near Fort Knyphausen (Fort Washington).[24] In that month
he was ordered across King's Bridge to work near a log house
between King's Battery (on Mrs. N. P. Bailey's place) and
Fort Number Seven (on Mr. Oswald Cammann's place). He
records that two English "Rehentschers" (Rangers) had been
hanged on two gallows, in front of the log house for murder.[25]
He was thus engaged during the winter, 1778-9, now on duty
on "Nord River Hill" (north of Spuyten Duivil), or in camp
under Fort Knyphausen—in dangerous proximity to the Blue
Bell tavern, at least judging so from the number of broils and
duels he was engaged in,—or detached on raids northward
through Yonkers, or at work on the redoubts on "Lourall
Hill" or at King's Battery.[26] While stationed on Laurel
Hill, he made a sketch of the view from there across the Harlem
River from Fort Number Eight on the south to Spuyten
Duyvil and the Hudson on the north.[27]

The winter quarters were uncomfortable. Nine huts were
provided for each company, which in summer were surrounded
with vegetable and flower gardens. Provisions were irregular
—there were no orchards to raid—and there was much suffering.[28] Some of the English troops had been sent to Oyster
Bay on Long Island for the winter months, to escape the
"exposed heights of King's Bridge," and returned in May,
1779.[29]

The British evidently found their redoubts beyond the Harlem River too scattered to be safe against the frequent raids of the Americans, and in August, 1779, they razed their works about King's Bridge, and removed their cannon and huts from Fort Independence.[330] Prince Charles Redoubt (on Marble Hill), however, was retained as the most northerly British post.[331] Redoubt Number Seven (on Mr. Oswald Cammann's place) was dismantled on September 10, 1779, and Redoubt Number Six (north of it) on the following day. The destruction of Fort Independence followed on September 12, 1779. A few days later King's Battery and Fort Number Five (on Mr. H. B. Claflin's place) were razed.[332] Part of the abattis from these dismantled redoubts was taken to Fort Number Eight for its repair. It was strengthened and garrisoned with one captain, one subaltern, and fifty privates.[333]

It was evidently General Knyphausen's plan to concentrate his troops about Fort Knyphausen, which was deemed "impregnable to the Rebels,"[334] and on Laurel Hill, which had been strengthened. Fort Number Eight was selected as the only redoubt to be retained beyond the Harlem River, as it lay within reach of the protecting guns of Fort George on Laurel Hill, and was connected with New York Island by a ferry (Howland's Ferry), leading from near the site of Morris Dock (to which a path led down from the fort) across to the creek opposite. A contemporary English writer says :[335] "On the east side of the East River, on the main land opposite to Laurel Hill, we have a work called Number Four (a mistake for Number Eight), in which is the only post we have on that side. In case of a serious attack it is probable we would abandon this post."

Fort Number Eight was useful in restraining the American raids in Westchester County. Heath writes :[336] "The enemy had a redoubt, called Number Eight, on the East Side of the Haerlem Creek, nearly opposite to the fort on Laurel Hill, and under fire of its cannon, for the security of their advanced troops on the Morrisania side."

The Americans were, in fact, constantly sweeping down on Morrisania, as, for instance, in August, 1779.[337] The boldness of their raids led to the strengthening of Fort Number Eight in the fall of 1779, fifty Hessians, among them our friend

Von Krafft, being detailed under Engineer Sproule for the purpose."[*]

Early in the fall the troops on the northern end of New York Island went into winter quarters. Von Krafft tells us that the winter was the coldest in twenty years. He was stationed in Fort Knyphausen, but was often detailed for active duty at Fort Number Eight, and occasionally at Cock Hill Fort on the heights south of Spuyten Duyvil, or in Prince Charles Redoubt (on Marble Hill) south of King's Bridge."[*]

The garrison at Fort Number Eight obtained their fuel from the woods back of their redoubt belonging to "a Rebel Colonel" (Colonel Richard Morris, grandfather of Mr. Lewis G. Morris). Major General von Lossberg and other generals lodged at his house at this time, in the absence of the family on their farm at Scarsdale."[*]

On February 2, 1780, Colonel Norton led a party of Hessians on a foraging expedition from King's Bridge to White Plains."[*] But the Americans did not leave such tactics to the British alone. In January, 1780, they attacked Colonel Hatfield in his quarters near the Benj. Archer house. This house, protected by the guns of Fort Number Eight, was at the time the headquarters of Colonel James DeLancey of the Royal Refugee Corps and of his notorious "Cow-Boys."[*] In May, 1780, they were surprised by some Massachusetts troops under Captain Cushing, who was guided to the Archer house by Michael Dykeman. Forty British soldiers were captured, but, fortunately for him, DeLancey was away at the time."[*]

These skirmishes occurred again in the following winter of 1780-1. In January, 1781, the Americans, under General Parsons, stole through the outposts at Morrisania and burnt DeLancey's camp near Fort Number Eight (presumably on the meadow, now the Berkeley Oval). They also cut the cable of Holland's Ferry leading to the foot of Laurel Hill, but were finally driven back."[*] During this year Von Krafft was still in camp near Fort Knyphausen, and at regular intervals stood guard at Fort Number Eight."[*] He also acted now and then as sentinel on Laurel Hill or on Cock Hill."[*]

This continual raiding by both American and British parties brought ruin and desolation to Westchester County. A French chaplain, writing from that region, in June, 1781, says:"[*] "as we approach towards New York, between the lines of both armies, we see more and more of the sorrowful vestiges of war and desolation,—the houses plundered, ruined and abandoned or burnt. . . . ."[144]

The most extensive of these raids was undertaken by Washington himself in the summer of 1781. He was aware that the British garrison in New York was weakened by large detachments being absent on foraging expeditions in New Jersey and further south. With some effort, Washington persuaded Rochambeau, the commander of the French troops which had reached Rhode Island, to join him in Westchester County, and menace the fortifications on the island of New York, and thereby compel the British to recall their troops from the south. The French moved slowly toward the rendezvous via Hartford and Newtown, Connecticut. Washington broke camp at New Windsor June 26, 1781, and moved to Peekskill.[149] The American army planned to attack Fort George on Laurel Hill, while the French, under the Duc de Lauzun, together with Sheldon's Dragoons and some Continental troops under Colonel Waterbury, were to surround and capture DeLancey's corps, encamped on the opposite bank of the river.[150]

On July 2, 1781, the Americans left Peekskill, and moved boldly to Valentine's Hill and the ruins of Fort Independence, some British skirmishers under Colonel Emerick retiring before them.[151] Here they were attacked by some Hessian troops, whom they first drove back towards King's Bridge. It is said that General Washington dined at the Van Cortlandt house on this occasion. Von Krafft records that the Americans were in full view (presumably from Laurel Hill) at the Van Cortlandt house.[152] Soon after, however, British reinforcements arrived, and the Americans had to retire from their position in Fort Independence.[153]

At the same time the French attack on the cantonments below Fort Number Eight was successfully met and repulsed by Colonel DeLancey's "Cow-Boys."[154] The return of the British troops from New Jersey and the appearance of English men-of-war in the Hudson off Spuyten Duyvil, compelled the immediate withdrawal of both armies to Yonkers, where Rochambeau joined Washington on July 10, 1781.[155] There

the two armies, numbering about 4,000 men, lay for ten
days, and then moved southward again, one column moving
off toward Throg's Neck and Morrisania to forage. The
other columns were drawn up on the heights back of Fort
Independence and stretching toward DeLancey's Mills (Bronxdale), Washington fixing his headquarters in Valentine's house
on Valentine's Hill, presumably the hill still known by that
name east of Yonkers and north of Woodlawn Cemetery.³⁰⁶

Those were lively days for the small garrison in Fort Number Eight and on Laurel Hill, as the entries in Von Krafft's
diary plainly show. They were in constant fear of being
attacked, and on July 22, 1781, could plainly see the Americans marching over what was formerly Fort Independence and
the dismantled King's Battery, where the gunners on Laurel
Hill tried to reach them with their cannon. Other columns of
Americans and a French regiment were seen marching behind
Fort Number Eight toward Morrisania (Mott Haven), where
they attacked the British outposts.³⁰⁷ Some Hessian Jägers
were sent across the Harlem River to reinforce the garrison
at Fort Number Eight, but the Americans and their allies
soon withdrew to North Castle, after a personal reconnoissance
of the British works by Rochambeau and Washington, which
no doubt convinced them that the British garrisons were too
strong for a direct assault—Abbé Robin thought they numbered 15,000—and that a siege was out of the question. The
plan of attacking New York was given up, and the last campaign of the war—the southern one—was begun, which was
to bring the revolution to a successful close.³⁰⁸

The skirmishes about Fort Number Eight continued. In
January, 1782, the Americans raided Morrisania once more,
but again they failed to capture Colonel DeLancey.³⁰⁹ In the
following month a similar raid was made, but with a similar
result.³¹⁰

In March, 1782, Captain Hunnewell and Major Woodbridge
led an attack upon DeLancey's camp near the Archer house.
In General Heath's words:³¹¹ "The horse proceeded down
between the British fort Number Eight and the cantonment of
DeLancey's corps, and having turned the cantonment between
daybreak and sunrise (March 4, 1782), they entered pell-

mell.'' The British were taken completely by surprise. The alarm gun at Fort Number Eight was fired, but, before reinforcements could be collected, the Americans had moved off towards East Chester.''[162] Ten days later they turned up at Mile Square, on the height east of the Hudson River and north of Fort Independence.[163]

These were the last movements of any importance about King's Bridge and Fort Number Eight. Heath records[164] that the British were demolishing their works at Fort Number Eight on November 20, 1782. The earthworks were still distinctly visible when the house now standing on the site of the fort was built in 1857.

Peace was assured at the end of 1782, but the other works were left garrisoned till the following year. In July, 1783, the embarkation of British troops for England and Nova Scotia began;[166] but not till November of that year were the British and Hessian troops withdrawn from the northern end of the island of New York.[166] Of these, parts of the following regiments had probably been at one time or another during the past seven years stationed at Fort Number Eight, as is shown by the buttons brought to light in digging on the site of the fort in 1857:

8th Regiment.

17th Regiment, in June, 1781, encamped below Cock Hill. Sent to Nova Scotia, 1783.[167]

33d Regiment, commanded by Lord Cornwallis, assisted at the assault on Laurel Hill, 1776. Sent to Nova Scotia, 1783.[168]

37th Regiment English Musketeers, commanded by Sir Eyre Coote, August 1781, encamped east of McGowan's Pass. Sent to Nova Scotia, 1783.[169]

38th Regiment. Returned to England, 1783.[170]

45th Regiment.

"R. P." "Erbprinz" Regiment (?)

74th Regiment. Returned to England, 1783.[171]

76th Scotch Regiment. In November, 1780, stationed at Prince Charles Redoubt, King's Bridge. Transferred to Laurel Hill a month later. Returned to England, 1783.[172]

By November 25, 1783, all British troops had left New York, and General Knox with a detachment of American

troops crossed King's Bridge and entered the city,[1] the first
to do so since the hasty evacuation by Washington seven years
before.

Peace had been practically established since the spring of
1783, and the Archers and other Westchester farmers could
now resume their peaceful vocations, and were rid for all time
of their unwelcome guests.

BIBLIOGRAPHY.

Abbé Robin (Chaplain in French Army), *New Travels through North America.* Boston, 1784.

Abstract of the Title of Cath'n E. Schwab to about 9 acres of land . . . in the manor of Fordham. The same of Henry W. T. Mali and of James Punnett. (Oelrichs & Co., 2 Bowling Green, N. Y.)

Adam, William, M.P., Conduct of the Present Administration, 1774–8. London, 1778.

Allen, Paul. History of the American Revolution. Baltimore, 1822.

American Archives, 5th Series, Washington, 1843–53.

Andrews, John. History of the War with America, France, Spain and Holland, 1775–1783. Vol. II, 1786.

Avery, David. Sermon preached at Norwich, Conn., Dec. 18, *1777.* Norwich, Conn., 1778.

Bancroft, Aaron. Life of George Washington. Worcester, 1807.

Bancroft, George. History of the United States. Boston, 1866. Vol. IX.

Barber, John W. Historical Collections of the State of New York. New York, 1851.

Blanchard, Claude, The Journal of. Commissary of the French Auxiliary Army, 1780–3. Translated by Wm. Deane. Albany, J. Munsell, 1876.

Bolton, Robert, Junior. History of the County of Westchester. New York, 1848.

Booth, Mary L. History of the City of New York. New York, 1866.

Botta, Carlo. Storia della Guerra dell' Independenza degli' Stati d'America. Milano, 1819. Tom. II.

(Burke, Edmund.) A History of . . . . the War in North America. London & Boston, 1780.

Calendar Historical Manuscripts relating to . . . the Revolution. Albany, N. Y., 1868.

Campaign of 1776, The. Memoirs Long Island Hist. Soc., III, 1878.

Carrington, H. B. Battles of the American Revolution. New York, 1876.

Carrington, H. B. Battle Maps and Charts of the American Revolution. New York.

Coghlan, Mrs. Memoirs of. New York, 1864.

Collections New York Historical Society for the year 1883. N. Y., N. Y. Hist. Society, 1884.

Connecticut Gazette, 1776.

Connecticut Journal, New Haven, Conn., 1776.

Curwen, Samuel. Journal and Letters of, 1775–83. Boston, 1864.

Dawson, Henry B. Westchester County, New York, During the Revolution. Morrisania, 1886.

———— —. *Westchester County, New York, During the American Revolution.* (Chap. VI in Scharf, Westchester County.)

———— —. *The Battle on Harlem Plains.* Valentine's Manual for 1868, p. 804.

Documents relating to the Colonial History of New York (B. Fernow, editor). Albany, N. Y., 1887.

Drake, F. S. Dictionary of American Biography. 2d Series. Boston, 1846.

Dunlap, William. History of . . . . the State of New York. New York, 1840.

Edsall, T. H. History of the Town of King's Bridge. New York, 1887.

———— —. *King's Bridge.* (Chap. XIX in Scharf, Westchester County.)

Eddis, William. Letters from America, 1769-1777. London, 1792.

Evidence on American War, Committee House of Commons, 3d edition. London, 1780.

Ellet, Mrs. The Domestic History of the American Revolution. New York, 1850.

Fisher, G. P. Life of Benjamin Silliman. New York, 1866.

Fiske, John. The American Revolution. Boston & New York, 1891.

Glass, Frances. Life of George Washington in Latin Prose. New York, 1835.

Glover, General John. A Memoir by William P. Upham, Salem, 1863.

(Gordon, P.) History of the War in America. Dublin, 1779.

(Graydon, Alexander.) Memoirs of a Life, chiefly in Pennsylvania. Edinburgh, 1822.

Graydon, Alexander. Memoirs of His Own Time (edited by J. S. Littell). Phila., 1846.

Greene, G. W. Life of Nathaniel Greene. New York, 1871.

(Hall, Captain.) History of the Civil War in America. London, 1780.

Heath, Major-General. Memoirs. Boston, 1798.

Hildreth, R. The History of the U. S. Vol. III. N. Y., 1882.

Histoire des troubles de l'Amérique Anglaise. Paris, 1787.

How, David. Diary. Morrisania, 1867.

Impartial History of the War in America. London, 1780.

Irving, Washington. Life of George Washington. New York, 1855; also, New York, 1883.

Jay, John. Battle of Harlem Plains. N. Y. Historical Society, 1876.

Johnson, William. Life and Correspondence of Nathaniel Greene. Charleston, 1822.

Johnston, H. P. The Campaign of 1776 around New York & Brooklyn. Memoirs of the Long Island Historical Society, vol. III, chap. 7. Brooklyn, 1878.

Jones, Thomas. History of New York during the Revolutionary War, (edited by E. F. DeLancey). New York, N. Y. Hist. Soc., 1879.

Jones, Thomas. Observations on New York, by H. P. Johnston. New York, 1880.

v. Krafft, J. C. Philip. Journal of Lieut., 1776-84. Collections N. Y. Hist. Soc., 1882-1883. p. 1.

Lamb, Mrs. Martha J. History of the City of New York. New York and Chicago, 1880.

Lamb, R. Journal of the American War. Dublin, 1809.

DeLancey, Edward F. Mount Washington and its Capture. Nov. 16, 1776. Magazine of American History, I, p. 65. New York, 1877.

The Lee Papers. Collections N. Y. Hist. Soc. for 1871-4.

Lossing, B. J. Pictorial Field-Book of the Revolution. New York, 1859.

Macaulcy, James. History of the State of New York. New York, 1829.

Magaw (Colonel) and the Fort Washington Captives. The American Historical Record, vol. II, p. 503. Jan., 1873.

Magazine of American History, vol. III, pp. 150, 152, Feb. 1879.

Marshall, Christopher, Extracts from the Diary of, (edited by W. Duane). Albany, 1877.

Marshall, Christopher, Diary, 1774-6, Phila., 1839, also Albany, 1877.

Marshall, John. Life of George Washington. Philadelphia, 1804.

Marshall, John. Life of George Washington. Philadelphia (*Atlas.*)

Minutes Supreme Executive Council of Pennsylvania, vol. XII. Harrisburg, 1853.

Minutes Supreme Executive Council of Pennsylvania, 2d Series, vol X. Harrisburg, 1852.

Montresor, J. Plan of the City of New York, 1766.

Moore, Frank. The Diary of the Revolution. Hartford, 1875. (Extracts from Whig and Tory newspapers.)

Morris, Fordham. Morrisania and West Farms. (Chaps. XXI-XXII in Scharf, Westchester County.

Murray, Rev. James. An Impartial History of the War in America. London, 1778, vol. II.

Nash, Solomon, Journal of, 1776-7. New York, 1861.

New York City during the American Revolution. Mercantile Library Association, 1861.

Pennsylvania Archives, 2d Series, vol. X. Harrisburg, 1880.

Pennsylvania Archives, vol. VII. Philadelphia, 1853.

The Political Magazine and Parliamentary . . . Journal for the year 1781.

Post, Mrs. Lydia Minturn. Recollections of the American Revolution. New York, 1859.

Ramsay, David. The History of the American Revolution. London, 1793.

The Remembrancer . . . for 1776. Part III. London, 1777; the same for 1778-9. London, 1779.

Rosengarten, J. G. The German Allied Troops in the North American War of Independence, 1776-83. (Translated by Max von Elking.) Albany, 1891.

Ruttenber, E. M. Obstructions to Navigation of Hudson's River. Albany, 1860.

Sabine, Lorenzo. Biographical Sketches of Loyalists of the American Revolution. Boston, 1864.

Scharf, J. T. History of Westchester County, vol. I. Phila., 1886.

Schwab, Gustav, Papers of Estate of. (Oelrichs & Co., 2 Bowling Green, N. Y.)

Simcoe, Colonel J. G. Military Journal. New York, 1844.

Smith, S. S. History of the United States. Philadelphia, 1818. vol. II.

Smith, William. History of New York. London, 1757.

Sparks, Jared. Library of American Biography. 2d Series. Boston, 1846.

Sparks, Jared. Correspondence of the American Revolution. Eminent Men to George Washington. Boston, 1853, vol. I.

Stedman, C. The History of the . . . American War. London, 1794.

Stevens, John A. The Operations of the Allied Armies before New York. 1781. Magazine of American History, IV, 1, Jan., 1880.

Stevens, John A. The Battle of Harlem Plains. Magazine of American History, IV, 331, May, 1880.

Stone, William L. Letters of Brunswick and Hessian Officers. Albany, 1891.

Tallmadge, Colonel Benjamin. Memoirs. New York, 1858.

Tomes, R. Battles of America. New York.

Warren, Mrs. Mercy. History . . . American Revolution. Boston. 1805.

Watson, John F. Historical Tales . . . of New York City and State. New York, 1832.

Watson, John F. Annals . . . of New York City. Philadelphia, 1846.

Webb, Samuel B., Correspondence and Journals of. vol. I, 1772-7. New York, 1893.

Webb, Samuel B. Reminiscences. New York, 1882.

Werthern, Freiherr von. Die hessischen Hülfstruppen im nordamerikanischen Unabhängigkeitskriege, 1776-83. Cassel, 1895.

Wilson, James G. Memorial History of the City of New York. New York, 1892. vol. II.

Year-Book, Society of Sons of the Revolution in the State of New York, 1893.

NOTES.

1. Abstract of Titles : Bolton, Westchester, II, 319, 328, 401 ; Scharf, Westchester County, I, 18, 33.
2. Ibid., 23, 66-7 ; Bolton, Westchester, II, 320, 406 ; Edsall, History King's Bridge, 63-5 ; Abstract of Titles.
3. Scharf, Westchester County, I, 24, 66, 68, 70-1, 744 ; Edsall, History King's Bridge, 4.
4. Ibid., 7, 63-7 ; Abstract of Titles ; Bolton, Westchester, II, 320 ; Scharf, Westchester County, I, 24, 71-2.
5. Bolton, Westchester, II, 319, 401 ; Abstract of Titles ; Scharf, Westchester County, I, 72, 96, 160.
6. Bolton, Westchester, II, 328-29.
7. Abstract of Titles ; Scharf, Westchester County, I, 778; Bolton, Westchester, II, 323.
8. Ibid., II, 324 ; Abstract of Titles.
9. Ibid.; Bolton, Westchester, II, 332 ; Smith, History N. Y., 196 ; Scharf, Westchester County, I, 756.
10. Abstract of Titles ; Bolton, Westchester, II, 328 ; Indenture, Oct. 14th, 1766, Schwab Estate, Papers.
11. Bolton, Westchester, II, 328, 333.
12. Bolton, Westchester, II, 328 ; Abstract of Titles ; Indenture Feb. 13th, 1769; ditto, April 12th, 1786, Schwab Estate, Papers.
13. Will Benjamin Archer, Schwab Estate, Papers; Abstract of Titles.
14. Ibid., Deeds March 17th, 1857, Schwab Estate, Papers.
15. Dawson, Westchester, 120; Scharf, Westchester County, I, 248-9, 255.
16. N. Y. during Am. Revolution, 120-37.
17. Scharf, Westchester County, I, 280; Doc's Colon. History N. Y., I. 135, 146, 169, 1306.
18. Ibid., I, 146; Dawson, Westchester, 103; Scharf, Westchester County, I, 278.
19. N. Y. during Am. Revolution, 120.
20. Wilson, History N. Y., II, 497, 500 ; N. Y. during Am. Revolution, 80; Webb, Reminiscenses, 38.
21. N. Y. during Am. Revolution, 97; compare Scharf, Westchester County, I, 340.
22. N. Y. during Am. Revolution, 29 ; Drake, Dict'y Am. Biogr., 262 ; Sabine, Loyalists, 363-5 ; Lossing, Field-Book, II, 624.
23. Irving, Washington, II, 364 ; Lossing, Field-Book, II, 624 ; Drake, Dict'y Am. Biogr., 262 ; N. Y. during Am. Revolution, 157-158 ; Sabine, Loyalists, 366.
24. Irving, Washington, IV, 296 ; Lossing, Field-Book, I, 753 (note), II, 624 ; Drake, Dict'y Am. Biogr., 262 ; Sabine, Loyalists, 369-70.

25. Simcoe, Journal, 17; Irving, Washington, II, 365-6; Wilson, History N. Y., II, 508.

26. Valentine's Manual for 1870, 805.

27. Wilson, History N. Y., II, 469.

28. Ibid., II, 473, 475; Mag. Am. History, III, 150, 152 (1879).

29. Wilson, History N. Y., II, 476.

30. Ibid., II. 500; N. Y. during Am. Revolution, 14; Montresor, Plan N. Y. City.

31. Smith, History N. Y., 196; compare Scharf, Westchester County, I, 30-1.

32. Barber, Hist. Coll'ns, N. Y., 356.

33. Lossing, Field-Book, II, 588.

34. Bolton, Westchester, II, 443-4.

35. Scharf, Westchester County, I, 800-1; Maps in N. Y. Historical Society; Carrington, Battle-Maps Am. Revolution, 20; Lossing Field-Book, II, 618; Wilson, History N. Y., II, 488, 523, 525; Valentine's Manual for 1854, 548, for 1859, 120, for 1861, 428; Mag. Am. History I, 2, 65 (1877); IV, 293, 304 (1880); Stedman, History Am. War, I, 210, 214; N. Y. during Am. Revolution; Campaign of 1776, appendix; Scharf, Westchester County, I, 402, 414.

36. Valentine's Manual for 1854, 362; for 1868, 812.

37. Ibid., for 1857, 208; Scharf, Westchester County, I, 472j.

38. Valentine's Manual for 1861.

39. Heath, Memoirs, 43; Lee Papers, I, 218.

40. N. Y. during the Am. Revolution, 88.

41. Ibid., 105.

42. Lee Papers, I, 235; compare Scharf, Westchester County, I, 324 & ss.

43. Ibid., I, 240, 268.

44. Ibid., I, 243; compare Scharf, Westchester County, I, 320-2.

45. N. Y. during Am. Revolution, I, 250, 259, 263.

46. Ibid., I, 337; N. Y. during Am. Revolution, 85-6.

47. Lee Papers, I, 272, 279, 354, 356.

48. Ibid., I, 337.

49. Heath, Memoirs, 52.

50. Lee Papers, I, 260, 322, 333-4, 337; Jones, History N. Y., I, 82-3.

51. Heath, Memoirs, 44, 46; Scharf, Westchester County, I, 330.

52. Lee Papers, I, 268; Wilson, History N. Y., II, 495.

53. Conn. Gazette, July 12, 1776; Delancey, Mount Washington, 69; Graydon, Memoirs, 151.

54. Penna. Archives, 2d Series, X, 103; Graydon, Memoirs, 178.

55. Delancey, Mount Washington, 69.

56. Penna. Archives, 2d Series, X, 156.

57. Graydon, Memoirs, 145, 147-8; Penna. Archives, 2d Series, X, 103.

58. Ibid., X, 103; Delancey, Mount Washington, 70.

59. Graydon, Memoirs, 177.

60. Heath, Memoirs, 47.

61. Wilson, History N. Y., II, 500-1; Glover, Memoir, 11; How, Diary, 23, 26.

62. Conn. Gazette, Aug. 23, 1776; Wilson, History N. Y., II, 500-1.
63. Lee Papers, I, 147.
64. DeLancey, Mount Washington, 66; Fisher, Silliman, I, 4.
65. N. Y. during Am. Revolution, 103.
66. Ibid., 71.
67. Ibid., 71 (note).
68. Ibid., 71.
69. Dawson, Westchester, 153; Scharf, Westchester County, I, 329.
70. DeLancey, Mount Washington, 68; Allen, Am. Revolution, I, 484.
71. Penna. Archives, 2d Series, X, 103; DeLancey, Mount Washington, 69; Heath, Memoirs, 52; Graydon, Memoirs, 148-9.
72. DeLancey, Mount Washington, 70.
73. Graydon, Memoirs, 178, 183.
74. Lossing, Field-Book, II, 610; Carrington, Battles Am. Revolution, 248.
75. Ibid., 248; Lossing, Field-Book, II, 610; Graydon, Memoirs, 191.
76. Lossing, Field-Book, II, 610.
77. Edsall, History King's Bridge, 26, 29, 30; Scharf, Westchester County, I, 11, 752-3.
78. Heath, Memoirs, 52; Edsall, History King's Bridge, 29, 30; Irving, Washington (1855), II, 233, 276.
79. Calendar Hist. MSS. Revn., II, 365-6.
80. Heath, Memoirs, 47, 49; Graydon, Memoirs, 150; Carrington, Battles Revolution, 243; Scharf, Westchester County, I, 383-4.
81. Heath, Memoirs, 44.
82. Ibid., 47-8; N. Y. during the Am. Revolution, 99; Lee Papers, I, 32.
83. Wilson, History N. Y., II, 496; N. Y. during Am. Revolution, 102; Lamb, Journal, 116; Lee Papers, I, 168.
84. Coghlan, Memoirs, 143; DeLancey, Mount Washington, 65.
85. Wilson, History N. Y., II, 507.
86. Stedman, History Am. War, I, 205; Scharf, Westchester County, I, 399-400.
87. Wilson, History N. Y., II, 507; Heath, Memoirs, 55; Dawson, Battle Harlem Plains, 804.
88. Am. Archives, 5th Series, I, 1489.
89. Ibid., 1502.
90. Heath, Memoirs, 53-4.
91. Lossing, Field-Book, II, 614; Carrington, Battles Am. Revolution, 221; Am. Archives, 5th Series, I, 1121-2.
92. Heath, Memoirs, 7, 10, 43, 46.
93. Am. Archives, 5th Series, I, 200; Heath, Memoirs, 56; Tallmadge, Memoir, 9; Impartial History War, 338.
94. Heath, Memoirs, 57; Lamb, Journal, 125; Dawson, Battle Harlem Plains, 805.
95. Heath, Memoirs, 57.
96. Ibid., 58.
97. Graydon, Memoirs, 170-1; How, Diary, 27.
98. Am. Archives, 5th Series, II, 106, 257, 259; Carrington, Battles Am. Revolution, 221.

99. Ibid., 220.
100. Am. Archives, 5th Series, II, 140.
101. Heath, Memoirs, 58.
102. Graydon, Memoirs, 171.
103. Am. Archives, 5th Series, II, 236-7.
104. Heath, Memoirs, 58.
105. Ibid., 58.
106. Ibid., 56; Scharf, Westchester County, I, 395.
107. Am. Archives, 5th Series, I, 1262.
108. Conn. Gazette, Sept. 20, 1776.
109. Am. Archives, 5th Series, II, 244; Heath, Memoirs, 59; N. Y. during Am. Revolution, 106.
110. Am. Archives, 5th Series, II, 274, 290; Heath, Memoirs, 59; Allen, Am. Revolution, I, 484; Wilson, History N. Y., II, 516.
111. Am. Archives, 5th Series, II, 267; Graydon, Memoirs, 171.
112. Nash, Journal, 32.
113. Am. Archives, 5th Series, II, 290.
114. Ibid., II, 699; Heath, Memoirs, 59; Lossing, Field-Book, II, 609; N. Y. during Am. Revolution, 106.
115. Carrington, Battles Am. Revolution, 224.
116. Nash, Journal, 33.
117. Heath, Memoirs, 60.
118. Jay, Battle Harlem Plains, 20; Lossing, Field-Book, II, 609.
119. Am. Archives, 5th Series, II. 299, 352; Allen, Am. Revolution, I, 484-6; Mag. Am. History, VIII, 40 (1882); Marshall, Diary, 105; Impartial History War, 347; Burke, History War, 217; Andrews, History War, 240; Lossing, Field-Book, II, 610; N. Y. during Am. Revolution, 111; Jones, History N. Y., I, 120; Wilson, History N. Y., II, 516.
120. Heath, Memoirs, 60; How, Diary, 28; Am. Archives, 5th Series, II, 699; Mag. Am. History, VIII, 40 (1882); Dawson, Battle Harlem Plains, 805; Lossing, Field-Book, II, 310.
121. Allen, History Am. Rev., I, 487; Dawson, Battle Harlem Plains, 806.
122. Am. Archives, 5th Series, II, 379; Jay, Battle Harlem Plains, 20; Gordon, History War, I, 192; Burke, History War, 218; Dawson, Battle Harlem Plains, 807.
123. Jay, Battle Harlem Plains, 20.
124. Am. Archives, 5th Series, II, 379; Dawson, Battle Harlem Plains, 807.
125. Heath, Memoirs, 60; Dawson, Battle Harlem Plains, 807-8; Nash, Journal, 34; DeLancey, Mount Washington, 75; N. Y. during Am. Revolution, 112.
126. How, Diary, 29.
127. Dawson, Battle Harlem Plains, map and 807-8.
128. Ibid., 808.
129. Ibid., 809-11.
130. Allen, History War, 488; Evidence, Am. War, 21.
131. Burke, History Am. Rev., 218; Mag. Am. History, VIII, 44 (1882), (Gen. Clinton to New York Convention.)

132. Impartial History War, 348; Andrews, History War, II, 241.
133. Hall, History War, I, 202; Eddis, Letters from Am., 331.
134. N. Y. during Am. Revolution, 109.
135. Heath, Memories, 62.
136. Ibid., 61-2; How, Diary, 31.
137. Ibid., 62.
138. Glover, Memoir, 15, 17; How, Diary, 29.
139. Heath, Memoirs, 63.
140. Penna. Archives, V, 27; Wilson, History N. Y., II, 515.
141. Conn. Gazette, May, 1776, et passim : (Advertisements of deserters).
142. Am. Archives, 5th Series, I, 1237.
143. Graydon, Memoirs, 172.
144. Am. Archives, 5th Series, I, 1272.
145. Heath, Memoirs, 63; Burke, History War, 218; Hildreth, History
     U. S., III, 153.
146. Heath, Memoirs, 63-6; Glover, Memoir, 17; How, Diary, 29; Daw-
     son, Westchester, 220; Scharf, Westchester County, I, 396.
147. How, Diary, 29.
148. Nash, Journal, 38.
149. Heath, Memoirs, 67-8.
150. Ibid., 67; Scharf, Westchester County, I, 408.
151. Webb, Correspondence, 169.
152. Am. Archives, 5th Series, II, 1188, III, 921-2; Heath, Memoirs, 70;
     Marshall, Extracts from Diary, 497; Impartial History War, 349;
     Johnston, Campaign 1776, 265; Wilson, History N. Y., II, 521;
     Dawson, Westchester, 231; Fiske, Am. Revolution, I, 217; Scharf,
     Westchester County, I, 406-7.
153. Anderson, History War, II, 243.
154. Carrington, Battles Am. Revolution, 234; Burke, History War, 219 :
     Hall, History War, I, 206; Allen, History Am. Revolution, I, 511.
155. Hall, History War, I, 203; Evidence Am. War, 21; Irving, Washing-
     ton (1855), II, 377; DeLancey, Mount Washington, 72-3.
156. Am. Archives, 5th Series, III, 921-2; Heath, Memoirs, 71; Burke,
     History War, 220; Dawson, Westchester, 240; Evidence Am. War,
     22-3.
157. Heath, Memoirs, 70; Scharf, Westchester County, I, 408.
158. Nash, Journal, 37.
159. How, Diary, 33.
160. Heath, Memoirs, 71.
161. Ibid., 71.
162. Ibid., 71; How, Diary, 33.
163. Am. Archives, 5th Series, II, 1130, 1167; III, 921-2; Heath, Memoirs,
     72; Nash, Journal, 37; How, Diary, 33; Stedman, History War, I,
     211 : Allen, History Am. Rev., I, 511; Wilson, History N. Y., II,
     521; Scharf, Westchester County, I, 417-19.
164. Heath, Memoirs, 72-3; How, Diary, 33.
165. Heath, Memoirs, 73.
166. Ibid., 66.

167. Ibid., 73; Lamb, Journal, 126; Lee Papers, IV, 288; Irving, Washington (1855), II, 399; Lossing, Field-Book, II, 615; Carrington, Battles Am. Revolution, 237; Scharf, Westchester County, I, 413.
168. Lee Papers, II, 283, 288.
169. Ibid., II, 203.
170. Ibid., II, 477.
171. Am. Archives, 5th Series, II, 1096-7, 1130; Conn. Gazette, Nov. 15, 1776.
172. Am. Archives, 5th Series, II, 1130.
173. Ibid., II, 1130; Heath, Memoirs, 73.
174. Am. Archives, 5th Series, III, 922; Nash, Journal, 38; Conn. Journal, Oct., 1776, also Nov. 6th, 1776; Burke, History War, 221; Andrews, History War, II, 244; Allen, History Am. Revolution, I, 512.
175. Heath, Memoirs, 73.
176. Am. Archives, 5th Series, II, 1130; Warren, History Am. Revolution; I, 326.
177. Am. Archives, 5th Series, II, 1130, III, 922; Heath, Memoirs, 73, 79: Adam, Present Administration, 24; DeLancey, Mount Washington, 75.
178. Heath, Memoirs, 79; Allen, History Am. Rev., I, 511.
179. Carrington, Battles Am. Rev., 242; Greene, Greene, I, 248; Dawson, Westchester, 257.
180. Am. Archives, 5th Series, II, 1294. (Gen. Greene to Gen. Washington, Oct. 31, 1776); Sparks, Correspondence, I, 299; Greene, Greene, I, 250.
181. Am. Archives, 5th Series, II, 1167; Allen, History Am. Rev., I, 512.
182. Calendar Hist. MSS. Revolution, I. 518.
183. Am. Archives, 5th Series, II, 1221; III, 922; Conn. Gazette, Nov. 15, 1776; Andrews, History War, II, 245; Allen, History Am. Revolution, I, 513.
184. Ibid., I, 513.
185. Ellet, Am. Revolution, chap. VI, 58 et ss.; Conn. Gazette, Nov. 15, 1776; Dawson, Westchester, 239.
186. Am. Archives, 5th Series, III, 922; How, Diary, 35; Impartial History War, 351-; Burke, History War, 222; Calendar Hist. MSS. Revolution, I, 532; Tallmadge. Memoir, 13; Andrews, History War, II, 245; Allen, History Am. Rev., I, 517; Histoire Troubles Am. Ang., I, 344; Carrington, Battles Am. Revolution, 239; Dawson, Westchester, 260; Wilson, History N. Y., II, 521.
187. Burke, History War, 224; Am. Archives, 5th Series, III, 922; Tallmadge, Memoir, 15; Lossing, Field-Book, II, 617; Scharf, Westchester County, I, 450.
188. Hall, History War, I, 210.
189. Post, Recollections, 34.
190. Wilson, History N. Y., II, 509; Coghlan, Memoirs, 150.
191. Watson, Hist. Tales, 192; Rosengarten, German Allied Troops, frontispiece; Hall, History War, I, 211.

192. Lossing, Field-Book, I, 321; Rosengarten, German Allied Troops, 189, 232.
193. Ibid., 23-4; Werthern, Hessische Hülfstruppen, 12.
194. Stone, Letters Brunswick and Hessian Officers, 188.
195. Am. Archives, 5th Series, III, 922; Lowell, Hessians in Rev., 75; Rosengarten, German Allied Troops, 45.
196. Am. Archives, 5th Series, III, 922; N. Y. Gazette & Weekly Mercury, Oct. 28, 1776.
197. Am. Archives, 5th Series, III, 922; The Remembrancer for 1776, III, 202.
198. Am. Archives, 5th Series, III, 922, 924; Murray, History War, II, 180; Hall, History War, I, 211; Allen, History Am. Revolution, I, 519; Burke, History War, 225; Carrington, Battles Am. Revolution, 242; Lossing, Field-Book, II, 619; Sparks, Correspondence, I, 302.
199. Rosengarten, German Allied Troops, 50.
200. The Remembrancer for 1776, III, 202; Am. Archives, 5th Series, III, 922.
201. Ibid., III, 547, 922; How, Diary, 36; The Remembrancer for 1776, III, 202; Heath, Memoirs, 84; Allen, History Am. Rev., I, 517; Carrington, Battles Revolution, 242; Scharf, Westchester County, I, 453.
202. Burke, History War, 224; Lossing, Field-Book, II, 617; DeLancey, Mount Washington, 77; Tallmadge, Memoir, 15; Evidence Am. War, 69; Scharf, Westchester County, I, 452.
203. Stedman, History Am. War, I. 216.
204. Am. Archives, 5th Series, III, 559, (Colonel Huntington to Gov. Trumbull, Nov. 7, 1776); Sparks, Correspondence, I, 302.
205. Heath, Memoirs, 83; Am. Archives, 5th Series, III, 556.
206. Evidence Am. War, 186.
207. Avery, Sermon, 1777.
208. Am. Archives, 5th Series, III, 541, 556, 837.
209. Ibid., III, 619.
210. Ibid., III, 556, 924; The Remembrancer for 1776, III, 202; Scharf, Westchester County, I, 453.
211. Greene, Greene, I, 261.
212. Moore, Diary, 341-3.
213. Am. Archives, 5th Series, III, 653, 674, 924; Nash, Journal, 40; Moore, Diary, 44; Hall, History War, I, 212; Andrews, History War, II, 247; Lee Papers, I, 273.
214. Am. Archives, 5th Series, III, 924; Heath, Memoirs, 85; The Remembrancer for 1776, III, 202; Burke, History War, 225; Scharf, Westchester County, I, 454.
215. Am. Archives, 5th Series, III, 924; The Remembrancer for 1776, III, 202; Dawson, Westchester, 278.
216. Am. Archives, 5th Series, III, 924; The Remembrancer for 1776, III, 202; Tomes, Battles Am., 386; Carrington, Battle Maps Revolution, 20; Carrington, Battles Am. Revolution, 249.

217. Am. Archives, 5th Series, III, 924; Graydon, Memoirs, 188; Marshall, Washington, II, 513; Jones, History N. Y., 632 (note); Edsall, History King's Bridge, 31; Impartial History War, 354; Burke, History War, 226; Johnson, Greene, 62; Bolton, Westchester, 336; Irving, Washington, II, 420; Stedman, History Am. War, I, 210; Lossing, Field-Book, II, 624; Carrington, Battles Revolution, 248; Carrington, Battle Maps Rev., 20; Mag. Am. History I, 65 (1877); IV, 293, 304 (1880).

218. Graydon, Memoirs, 198.

219. Stedman, History War, I, 216-7; Bancroft, History U. S., IX, 189.

220. Ibid., IX, 189; Am. Archives, 5th Series, III, 706-7; The Remembrancer for 1776, III, 203.

221. Am. Archives, 5th Series, III, 924; Mag. Am. History, I, 65 (1877).

222. Am. Archives, 5th Series, III, 924; The Remembrancer for 1776, III, 203; Hall, History War, 214; Burke, History War, 225-6; Carrington, Battles Revolution, 248; Carrington, Battle Maps Revolution, 20; Wilson, History N. Y., II, 488, 509, 525; Valentine's Manual for 1854, 548, for 1859, for 1861, 120; Stedman, History War, I, 210, 214; DeLancey, Mount Washington, 65; Mag. Am. History, IV, 2, 293, 304 (1880).

223. Am. Archives, 5th Series, III, 924; Burke, History War, 226-7; Carrington, Battles Revolution, 248.

224. Am. Archives, 5th Series, III, 924.

225. Carrington, Battles Revolution, 249.

226. Am. Archives, 5th Series, III, 548; Sparks, Correspondence, 298.

227. Penna. Archives, 2d Series, X, 103, 565.

228. Penna. Archives, 2d Series, X, 140-1.

229. Am. Archives, 5th Series, III, 706-7; Graydon, Memoirs, 178.

230. Carrington, Battles Revolution, 243; Drake, Dict'y. Am. Biogr., 592; Magaw & Ft. Washington, 304; DeLancey, Mount Washington, 69; Penna. Archives, 2d Series, X, 142; Minutes Provincial Council Penna., X, 124, 442-3, 490.

231. Am. Archives, 5th Series, III, 693; Graydon, Memoirs, 194.

232. Ibid., 189, 199; Johnson, Greene, 61, 63; Irving, Washington, II, 420; Lossing, Field-Book, II, 610, 620.

233. Carrington, Battles Revolution, 248.

234. Am. Archives, 5th Series, III, 674; Lamb, Journal, 126.

235. Am. Archives, 5th Series, III, 793; Greene, Greene, I, 263.

236. Carrington, Battles Revolution, 243; Ruttenber, Obstructions Hudson, 38, 50, 51.

237. Am. Archives, 5th Series, II, 236-7; Nash, Journal, 36; Heath, Memoirs, 68.

238. Nash, Journal, 37.

239. Lee Papers, II, 289.

240. Carrington, Battles Revolution, 249.

241. Graydon, Memoirs, 219; (quoted in note by E. F. DeLancey in Jones, History N. Y., I, 629-630; also in Littell's edition, 215.)

242. DeLancey, Mount Washington, 80; the same, note in Jones, History N. Y., I, 630-1.

243. Jones, History N. Y., I, 631, note.
244. Lamb, History N. Y., II, 142; Johnston, Campaign 1776, 281; Wilson, History N. Y., II, 522, note.
245. Jones, History N. Y., I, 632, note; Penna. Archives, 2d Series, X, 145.
246. Ibid., 140, 142; Minutes Provincial Council Penna. X, 499.
247. Penna. Archives, 2d Series, X, 141.
248. Jones, History N. Y., I, 628-9.
249. DeLancey, Mount Washington, 77-9.
250. Wilson, History N. Y., II, 522, note.
251. Coll'ns N. Y. Hist. Soc., 1883, 512.
252. Jones, History N. Y., I, 626, note.
253. Original material: Am. Archives, 5th Series, III, 706-7, 793, 924-5; Graydon, Memoirs, 200-9; The Remembrancer for 1776, III, 203; Eddis, Letters, 336-7; Moore, Diary, 345; Conn. Gazette, Nov. 29, 1776; Heath, Memoirs, 85; Dunlap, History N. Y., II, 79-88; Penna. Archives, 2d Series, X, 105; Lee Papers, II, 279 (Gen. Washington to Gen. Lee, Nov. 16, 1776); II, 284. Based on original material: Johnston, Campaign 1776, 276-; Carrington, Battle Maps Revolution, 20; Carrington, Battles Revolution, 250; Lossing, Field-Book, II, 620-; DeLancey, Mount Washington, 82-; Lowell, Hessians in Rev. War, 79-; Full accounts: Lamb, Journal, 128; Gordon, History War, I, 197; Hall, History War, I, 215-; Andrews, History War, II, 248; Stedman, History Am. War, I, 217-; Marshall, Washington, II, 514-; Ramsay, History Am. Revolution, II, 309; Smith, History U. S., II, 135; Tomes, Battles Am., 385-; Botta, Storia della Guerra, II, 393; Allen, History Am. Revolution, I, 520-; Macaulay, History N. Y., III, 153-; Sparks, Washington, 199-; Bancroft, Washington, I, 118-; Irving, Washington, II, 419-; Histoire des troubles Am. Ang., I, 349-; Booth, History N. Y., 507-; Lamb, History N. Y., II, 142-; Wilson, History N. Y., II, 524-; Impartial History War, 354-; Meagre Accounts: Warren, History N. Y., I, 333; Fiske, Revolution, I, 220; Jones, History N. Y., I, 124-; Werthern, Hessische Hülfstruppen, 17-.
254. Graydon, Memoirs, 199.
255. Ibid., 194.
256. Ibid., 193.
257. Ibid., 195.
258. Carrington, Battle Maps Am. Rev., 20; The Remembrancer for 1776, III, 203; Am. Archives, 5th Series, III, 924.
259. Heath, Memoirs, 85; Am. Archives, 5th Series, III, 707.
260. Bancroft, History U. S., IX, 190.
261. Rosengarten, German Allied Troops, 51.
262. Am. Archives, 5th Series, III, 751, 765, 925; Graydon, Memoirs, 197, 201; Hall, History War, I, 214; Allen, History Am. Rev., I, 522; Carrington, Battle Maps Am. Rev., 20; N. Y. Gazette & Weekly Mercury, Nov. 25, 1776.
263. Am. Archives, 5th Series, III, 925; Carrington, Battles Revolution, 250.

264. Bolton, Westchester, II, 337.
265. Am. Archives, 5th Series, III, 707 ; Bancroft, History U. S., IX, 191;
    The Remembrancer for 1776, III, 203 ; Tomes, Battles Am., 390 ;
    Burke, History War, 225 ; Stedman, History War, I, 218 ; Lamb
    Journal, 128 ; Allen, History Am. Rev., I, 521 ; Lossing, Field-
    Book, II, 620.
266. Graydon, Memoirs, 203.
267. Heath, Memoirs, 85.
268. Am. Archives, 5th Series, III, 924.
269. Lossing, Field-Book, II, 621.
270. Carrington, Battles Am. Rev., 250.
271. DeLancey, Mount Washington, 87.
272. Johnston, Greene, I, 63.
273. Gordon, History War, I, 198 ; Impartial History War, 355.
274. Murray, History War, II, 181.
275. Graydon, Memoirs, 201 ; Hall, History War, I, 215 ; Burke, History
    War, 226-7 ; Carrington, Battles Rev., 250 ; DeLancey, Mount
    Washington, 87.
276. Am. Archives, 5th Series, III, 924 ; Graydon, Memoirs, 196 ; Allen,
    History Am. Rev., I, 521-2, 524 ; Carrington, Battle Maps Am.
    Rev., 20.
277. Conn. Gazette, Nov. 29, 1776.
278. Am. Archives, 5th Series, III, 924; Heath, Memoirs, 85 ; Allen, His-
    tory Am. Rev., I, 522; Carrington, Battle Maps Rev., 250.
279. Am. Archives, 5th Series, III, 707.
280. Irving, Washington, II, 423.
281. Am. Archives, 5th Series, III, 311 ; Heath, Memoirs, 85 ; The Re-
    membrancer for 1776, III, 204 ; Tallmadge, Memoir, 15 ; Conn.
    Gazette, Nov. 29, 1776 ; Lossing, Field-Book, II, 621 ; Penna.
    Archives, 2d Series, X, 105 ; Lee Papers, I, 279 (Washington to
    Lee, Nov. 16, 1776).
282. Francis, Washington, 77 (note) ; Sparks, Am. Biogr., 2d Series, X,
    44.
283. Am. Archives, 5th Series, III, 311.
284. Ibid., III, 855-6.
285. Ibid., III, 1058.
286. Graydon, Memoirs, 208-9.
287. Rosengarten, German Allied Troops, 52 ; Carrington, Battle Maps
    Rev., 20.
288. Am. Archives, 5th Series, III, 730.
289. Marshall, Extracts Diary, 104 ; Marshall, Diary, 117.
290. How, Diary, 36.
291. Conn. Journal, Nov. 20, 1776.
292. Ibid., Nov. 27, 1776.
293. Curwen, Journal, 100.
294. Magaw and Fort Washington, 504.
295. Am. Archives, 5th Series, III, 855-6.
296. N. Y. Gazette & Weekly Mercury, Nov. 25, 1776.

297. Am. Archives, 5th Series, III, 751.
298. Ibid., III, 856 ; Lee Papers, II, 315.
299. Heath, Memoirs, 103 ; Calendar Hist. MSS. Rev., I, 670 ; Carrington, Battle Maps Rev., 20; Lossing, Field-Book, II, 620.
300. Moore, Diary, 378-9; Irving, Washington (1883), IV, 8, 109, 273;
Post, Recollections, 55 ; Lossing, Field-Book, II, 624.
301. Heath, Memoirs, 103-8 ; Moore, Diary, 400; Lossing, Field-Book, II,
624-5.
302. Lossing, Field-Book, II, 623 ; Scharf, Westchester County, I, 753-4;
Heath, Memoirs, 109.
303. Ibid., 110-2.
304. Ibid., 113 ; Edsall, History King's Bridge, 33.
305. Heath, Memoirs, 115.
306. Lossing, Field-Book, I, 762 (note).
307. Simcoe, Journal, 76-80.
308. Ibid., 79 ; Bolton, Westchester, II, 445.
309. Simcoe, Journal, 101-2.
310. Ibid., 74-5 ; Rosengarten, German Allied Troops, 159.
311. Simcoe, Journal, 83, 105 ; Von Krafft, Journal, 57.
312. Simcoe, Journal, 74.
313. Ibid., 88 ; Rosengarten, German Allied Troops, 160.
314. Lee Papers, I, 11.
315. Simcoe, Journal, 80-6 ; Scharf, Westchester County, I, 755.
316. Watson, Annals, N. Y., 328 ; Von Krafft, Journal, x-xi.
317. Ibid., 52-4.
318. Ibid., 54.
319. Ibid., 54.
320. Ibid., 56-8.
321. Ibid., 60.
322. Ibid., 64-5.
323. Ibid., 65-8.
324. Ibid., 69, 72.
325. Ibid., 73.
326. Ibid., 75, 78, 80, 82, 84.
327. Ibid., 201 (plate VI); Wilson, History N. Y., II, 525; Valentine,
Manual for 1854, 548.
328. Von Krafft, Journal, 74; Rosengarten, German Allied Troops, 171.
329. Simcoe, Journal, 93, 101.
330. Heath, Memoirs, 214; Penna. Archives, VII, 636 ; Von Krafft, Journal, 90.
331. Polit. Mag. & Parl. Journal, 1781, 658.
332. Edsall, History King's Bridge, 30-1 ; Von Krafft, Journal, 93-4.
333. Ibid., 94.
334. Edsall, History King's Bridge, 658.
335. Polit. Mag. & Parl. Journal, 1781, 657-8.
336. Heath, Memoirs, 223.
337. Ibid., 215, 223.
338. Von Krafft, Journal, 96.

339. Ibid., 103, 122-5.
340. Ibid., 123.
341. Irving, Washington (1883), IV, 8.
342. Lossing, Field-Book, II, 624; Bolton, Westchester, II, 336.
343. Ibid., II, 333; Lossing, Field-Book, II, 624; Irving, Washington (1883), IV, 273.
344. Bolton, Westchester, II, 334; Heath, Memoirs, 272; Moore, Diary, 905-9; Von Krafft, Journal, 130.
345. Ibid., 129-33, 140, 143, 146, 148, 150.
346. Ibid., 113, 151, 190.
347. Robin, Travels, 28.
348. Compare Irving, Washington (1883), IV, 8, 109.
349. Stevens, Allied Armies, 2-4; Lossing, Field-Book, II, 625-6; Irving, Washington, IV, 306; Marshall, Washington, I, 445-6; Blanchard, Journal, 109, 111; N. Y. during Am. Rev., 177.
350. Stevens, Allied Armies, 6; N. Y. during Am. Rev., 177; Lossing, Field-Book, II, 626.
351. Moore, Diary, 979; Lowell, Hessians in Rev. War, 260.
352. Von Krafft, Journal, 142-3; Lossing, Field-Book, II, 623.
353. Blanchard, Journal, 119, 121; N. Y. during Am. Rev., 180; Moore, Diary, 980-1; Lowell, Hessians in Rev. War, 261; Stevens, Allied Armies, 7-9; Edsall, History King's Bridge, 41.
354. Stevens, Allied Armies, 9; Sabine, Loyalists, I, 370.
355. Blanchard, Journal, 120; Stevens, Allied Armies, 10; Lossing, Field-Book, II, 626; Robin, Travels, 30.
356. Stevens, Allied Armies, 23; Von Krafft, Journal, 143; N. Y. during Am. Rev., 181.
357. Von Krafft, Journal, 143, 145; Blanchard, Journal, 123.
358. Ibid., 120, 127; N. Y. during Am. Rev., 182; Stevens, Allied Armies, 24; Robin, Travels, 33, 36; Heath, Memoirs, 295.
359. Ibid., 326.
360. Ibid., 329.
361. Ibid., 329.
362. Bolton, Westchester, II, 334; Lossing, Field-Book, II, 624.
363. Heath, Memoirs, 331.
364. Ibid., 357; Bolton, Westchester, II, 337.
365. Von Krafft, Journal, 190; N. Y. during Am. Rev., 141.
366. Wilson, History N. Y., II, 554; Irving, Washington, IV, 438; Post, Recollections, 55; N. Y. City during Am. Rev., 157-.
367. Von Krafft, Journal, 126, 132, 190; Valentine's Manual for 1870, 804.
368. Von Krafft, Journal, 190; Valentine's Manual for 1870, 804.
369. Von Krafft, Journal, 95, 148, 190; Valentine, Manual for 1870, 804.
370. Ibid., 804; Von Krafft, Journal, 126, 139, 147, 190.
371. Ibid., 190; Valentine, Manual for 1870, 804.
372. Ibid., 804; Von Krafft, Journal, 124-5.
373. Hildreth, History U. S., III, 441.